I Am Homeless If This Is Not My Home

ALSO BY LORRIE MOORE

See What Can Be Done

Bark

A Gate at the Stairs

Birds of America

Who Will Run the Frog Hospital?

Like Life

Anagrams

Self-Help

I AM
HOMELESS
IF THIS IS NOT
MY HOME

Lorrie Moore

faber

This export edition first published in the UK in 2023
by Faber & Faber Limited
The Bindery
51 Hatton Garden
London EC1N 8HN

First published in the United States in 2023
by Alfred A. Knopf, a division of Penguin Random House LLC, New York 1745
Broadway New York NY, 10019
www.aaknopf.com

Printed and bound in the UK by CPI Group (UK) Ltd, Croydon CR0 4YY

A CIP record for this book
is available from the British Library

ISBN 978–0–571–27386–7

2 4 6 8 10 9 7 5 3 1

For my sister and my brothers

The buckwheat cake was in her mouth . . .

STEPHEN FOSTER, "Oh! Susanna"

The animal magnetism of a dead body makes the stress come slanting, so the seams and joints of a coffin are made on the bevel.

WILLIAM FAULKNER, *As I Lay Dying*

We live in an age of some really great blow-job artists. Every era has its art form. The nineteenth century, I know, was tops for the novel.

SHEILA HETI, *How Should a Person Be?*

I Am Homeless If This Is Not My Home

D^{earest} Sister,
      The moon has roved away in the sky and I don't even know what the pleiades are but at last I can sit alone in the dark by this lamp, my truest self, day's end toasted to the perfect moment and speak to you. Such peace to have the house quiet—outside I believe I hear the groaning deer. The wild-eyed varmints in the traps are past wailing, and the nightjars whistle their hillbilly tunes. I can momentarily stop pretending to tend to my accounts in the desk cartonnier. The gentleman lodger who is keen to relieve me of my spinsterhood has gone upstairs to bed, clacking his walking stick along the rails of the banister, just to create a bit of tension; now overhead his footfall to and from the basin squeaks the boards. I have a vague affection for him, which is not usable enough for marriage. I cannot see what he offers in that regard, despite some impressively memorized Shakespeare and Lord Byron and some queerly fine mimicry of the other lodgers: Priscilla the plump quakeress, tragically maddened by love. Miriam with her laryngitis and Confederate widow's weeds (the town has run out of that slimming black silk and resorts to a confused dark Union blue). Or Mick, the old

Chickasaw bachelor, who keeps a whole hawk wing pinned to his never-doffed cowboy hat.

Dapper as a finch, the handsome lodger can also recite the bewildering poems of Felicia Hemans, one of which features a virtuous heroine torn from home by pirates—sweet Jesus take the reins. His mustache is black and thick as broom bristle and the words come flying out from beneath it like the lines of a play in a theater on fire. He has an intriguing trunk of costumes in his closet—cotton tights, wool tights, a spellbinding number of tights, some wigs he combs out and puts on for amusement, and even some stuffing for a hunchback which he portrays unnervingly and then lets the stuffing fall completely out. I don't know how he could manage a vigorous sword fight wearing those wigs. If I don't laugh he puts it all away. He says he suffers stage fright everywhere but the stage. He says he will help me build a platform on the side of the house, if I would like to get into wicked show business and put great joy into the hearts of simple men.

"I will certainly think about that," say I and go about my chores.

"Why, Miss Libby, an Elizabeth should learn Elizabethan."

"Should she now."

"I do desire that we be better strangers." He is bold.

But he has his own straitened circumstances which I hardly need to take on as my own, though he appears always in fine fettle—handsome in the silvery variegated fashion of rabbits and foxes, a pair of pomaded muttonchops which he says hide a bite scar from his boyhood horse, Cola. The muttonchops fetchingly collect snow in January, though he limps—some might say *imperceptibly* but that has the lie built right in, so I don't say that, not being a good liar. A cork foot from the secesh, he told me. Mounted the real foot and donated it to a Lost Cause Army

Medical Museum, he said, and sometimes he goes and visits it just to say hello. Well, everyone got a little too dressed up for that cause, I do not reply, claret-capes and ostrich plumes, as if they were all in a play, when they should instead have noted that causes have reasons they get themselves lost. The smash comes soon enough, as others have declared, and a boy's adventures know no pity. These dazed old seceshers are like whittlers who take small sticks and chop them away, making nothing but pixie pollen. I find people's ideas are like their perfume—full of fading then dabbing on again—with no small hint of cidered urine. A good scalawag sticks to the late night cipher of her diary. Also? I myself have taken to whittling and am making your Eliza a doll from some spruce wood. Its body is like a star and I will sew it a dress out of an old Indian blanket and it will look exactly like some doddering namesake aunt made it for her.

From time to time I detect some craftiness about this particular lodger and his less than gallant crumbs of bluster. But he can blow a whistle with his eye—no small matter. He sings, "I Used to Be Lucky but Now I'm Not." Then does that whistle out his eye.

Ha! He told me all of his people were actors, that a family of actors was not only the best strategy for the future of American drama but would eventually be its greatest subject! at which I scowled. Then he said not really, but some of his kin were in fact politicians who conducted themselves like actors, one of them once banished to a prison ship, though another brother Ned now mingled with high society. I tried to unclench my mind and free my felt scowl into mock surprise. Then he told me the truth: he had spent years in the circus, after his quinine smuggling for the secesh. Ha again!

"Do I jar you?" he asks with his sly charm.

"No," I say. "I am braced at every turn for disenchantment."

"Well that might be just a little too bad," he says. His look is like last year's bird's nest.

"Simply saying."

"I understand," he said.

He claims I have inner beauty.

"I wish it would strike outward," I replied. "It's best to have things come to the surface." Among his papers upstairs I have noted letters from female admirers whose signatures he has removed with a razor. A gentlemanly mutilation, I suppose, preserving their privacy.

Well, Lucifer himself was surely a gentleman: he would have needed such manners to get around.

My lodger rhymes *again* with *rain*—what is the point of that? Still, I am afraid I'm too often glad of his company. Thus he has full board at a kind price, plus my bettermost chamber, the brass bed with the Job-tears quilt, the cabinetted tub, and the window with only the one paper pane, the rest being glass ambrotypes of crippled young men which I found on the curb outside a retired war surgeon's house. They fit nicely between the cames. When the enlivening light shines through them, in rose and gray, it breaks your heart.

Charity, our mother used to say, is more virtuous than love, and in some languages the same. Desire, of course, on my part has been shooed away by the Lord. Though sometimes I think I see it, raggedy, out back among the mossy pavers, like a child cutting across yards to get to school. One sees a darting through the gum trees and hickories that have come back from the winter's scorching freeze. Oh, yes, I say to the darting thing, the fluff of a dandelion clock or a milkweed puff: I sort of remember you.

Now as I write, a fierce rain has begun to fall on the roof. The owls in the garden will suffer, their wings having to dry to fly. Honey, I have sent your Harry a birthday letter and a gray-back with pretty Lucy Pickens on the front. I have heard Miss Pickens was mad as a dog and vain as a cat, but every type of money and mindset is still permissible here. If no bank up there will take the grayback he will have to put it in a scrapbook. You never know what will become a collector's item—words to be carved on my headstone. Also, REST YOUR HORSE AND BUGGY HERE—that one for visitors, there being no graveside ostler. *Hold your own horses,* if I'm not as ready as I expect to be. I have also sent Harry some old rebel coins for pounding into cufflinks.

Though greenbacks are preferred, I still will take from my lodgers whatever the savings and loan will accept, even the new Canadian money which is coursing about, though I would pre-fer some wampum or a beaver pelt and am not above taking jewelry, since the Union men, and everyone posing as Union men, are having trouble getting their pension pay. I take silver ingots or rhinestone buttons or large sea shells if they are pretty and you can hear the sea. All is tradable somewhere because we live in a forgotten way in some corner of the beginning of the end of the beginning. I don't know who I really mean by "we." But it does seem this place has been handed some moment in history then grown fearful and impulsive about hanging on to it. A useless lunge. Sinful even. A good scalawag sticks to her diary. As I said.

Once in a while the river floods, giving us the sense that we have once more got to sacrifice before we can start over yet again. I'm grateful my house is on a hill, high above South Sunken

Road and a better place from which to pretend to see you. And why is it pretending? Occasionally I know I do. I am here for you and with you. Transportation to be determined. When the clouds swirl and marble the night sky like meat fat, the antimacassars on the clothesline, not taken down at night, flip up in the wind and are my fretted firmament and all my stars. I look through them and on up into the trees, which carve the horizon like a jigsaw. Peek through, sister mine.

Someone at the pots and pans store was speaking of a neighbor woman who has become a bitter old recluse and I piped up that that was going to be my own fate and no one kindly took it upon themselves to disabuse me. Everyone simply stared in bright-eyed agreement. I fear they have seen me muttering to myself on the street. Once, I swaddled a burn on my arm with a dressing, and then when I was out walking began to swat at it, thinking it was a large moth that had wrapped itself around me. I should wear a duster and one of the new pancake hats that are all the rage. I should take up ornamental farming with guano. When I have my visits with the pastor, our Saturday tea in my own front parlor, it strikes me that he is the lone soul to try to argue me into a more cheerful condition. "What is there to be bitter about?" the pastor asks me. And I say, rudely stitching up a nine-patch quilt right in front of him, "Well, sir, to take the long way around the barn, I don't always know, but I do *feel* there's much: I cannot see life, what it's supposed to be: I'm stumped and mystified and frozen in place. Yet other times, I realize, regardless, there's a lot to be thankful for. It's perplexing! How's a soul to know?" And he looks sidelong at the floor and chuckles as if I've once again accomplished the pointless feat of outsmarting a man of God at cards. But I am the empty-handed one. I am the dummy—a card-playing word I've picked up from the courting lodger who has taught me a new game from India or Canada or Australia. He has been to all. I am the partner of the declarer, says lodger Jack with a wink, as he essentially plays the game himself—I prefer Whist or Faro—with me saying, "What do I do now?" Which stands for the whole thing. But also makes me wonder about the pastor's other calls. They must be dirt-dull and full of pitiful sick people for him to linger with me and my spiritual paralysis. In the afternoon he swirls the tea around and pretends to read the leaves. "God has plans for you."

"To wash the dishes," I say, already weary of God's plans. Once the handsome lodger passed briskly by in a velvet cape, out the door for his walk, touching his wide-brimmed hat in our direction, while the pastor was there in the receiving parlor with me but we paid little heed to one another. Another time the lodger, in a topcoat blue as crab blood, breezed out and I said to the pastor, "He's a flouncer."

Or else if the lodger casts a disapproving eye, I say to the pastor, "He's a Catholic." But when I have to say nothing at all, all three of us wordlessly and indulgently appear to understand everything, and for a moment life has grace. Unlike those moments when the lodger strolls past, finds me alone, and twirls his cane at me then fires it like a shotgun.

People don't think I know who they are. But as mistress of this house I sometimes have a lead on things.

How I miss you still. The other day I remembered how we would sneak into the match satchel and suck on the blown out ones, getting all the crazy juice out of them, craving some mineral or other, and then line our eyes with the blackened tips. And so I did it again just to see how it would make me look today and all I can say is this town has no need of yet another home-made Cleopatra. Although I would look right nice with a big old snake dangling from my breast. Done in by the copperheads just says it all. Everything says everything, and all says all.

I have reached a tiredness with the housekeeping and so the whole place has lost its spank. Most weekends and holidays I cold harbor it and the lodgers find their meals elsewhere, usually down the road at Wilmer's. And though Ofelia still comes by to help with the laundry, and place the wash water out in a basin for the thirsty, fatally curious squirrels, and bring in new water from the well and heat it up on the hob, it is never enough. On Mondays, despite the handsome lodger's request for baked duck (the buckshot would crack a tooth), Ofelia puts a calf head or a hambone in a soup pot and boils away, adding a tin of turnips, every last shuck and nubbin of leftover corn, an age-old can of goober peas. To supplement there is a yam cake, a cottage cheese pie, a cabbage from Mr. Stanley Woo's cart. Once a month she makes a quite gruesome hog maw which we eat for days. For breakfast I take a banana and in the center of everybody's oatmeal place a single slice, so they can look at its man-in-the-moon face. The floors grow smudgy and the cornbread dry—good for a panade. I can hardly tell you what I do with the squirrels (well, all right: I drown them with a contraption like a see-saw that dumps them in a tub of water—harder with a duck—and then you whack them if they don't fully drown) but at least the stews don't have pellets in them. Maybe a soapsud or two but not in a way that you would notice unless perhaps one suddenly feels one's conscience a little cleaner.

But all is wearying here at South Sunken Road. I remove a cobweb, and another one soon springs up wide and eery as a fairy hand. The flour moths flicker in and out of the cupboards and I let them. I have not got a good handle on the grandfather clock and sometimes would rather see an actual grandfather standing there than see that mechanical face spinning like a mad devil not telling you how it does what it does. Whereas an old man will tell you everything.

When I go back to the places of the past, nothing is there anymore, as if I have made the whole thing up. It is as if life were just a dream placed in the window to cool, like a pie, then stolen. Those are the moments that I then sit and imagine you and wonder what you would say. Reminiscence is an earache, you would declare. Although I suppose I myself am a type—brooding, prim, not as Christian as I pretend, anti-madamic, as the courting gentleman has remarked. Many of my lodgers—the card players and magicians, the bushwhackers, Jews, and Shawnees—are filled up with the new culture: electricity, railroads, hot air balloons, and the western desert still contriving one silver rush after gold then silver again perhaps for more pictures of soldiers and wars, causing everyone to bust out on a boyish freak for a place with Dust or Butte or Scratch in its name, hooting and humming and carrying the large load of their former and perishing hearts, everybody going farther than they should. The Westward Ho of the disabused soldier. There is now a wooden sidewalk on our main street that is good for getting them there—three blocks worth at any rate. The whiff of boondoggle is in the air. Yesterday I saw a large credulous sow trotting down the wheel-rutted road as if it had heard tell of something and eaten her litter so as to be free to investigate. Though probably she would end up gorging on some forgotten boy's body in some field after the rain somewhere. The farmers' pigs still root up dead soldiers in the ground. You don't even have to be near a battlefield for that. Some of these boys were deserters and stragglers and all were hungry and shot and now years later rummaged for as livestock feed.

As for the Westward Ho, many of those towns are likely not to take. A hub can turn into the end of the line, even for a credulous hog evading Ofelia's maw. But there is no disenthralling a determined creature! let alone these grizzled mystery men with their secrets and gold necklaces and their money to pay a dentist to pull out all their teeth once they hear of some mecca somewhere—Dimmit River, Turkey Miller's Plum, and suchlike. It all threatens to become a limbo when rumors and auguries of other heavens blow in. Some of these gentlemen have become stationary spectators, having stopped their restless movements some time ago—their hearts no longer consulted. Although no one's heart gets consulted on much, bedeviled, dragged behind, twitching.

Well, darlin girl, sorrow and bitterness must be pushed past, and when one stops to look about, there life is! an inland sea in a landlocked place, the world again ready to barkle you with its fossils and warts and other unwanted larksome gifts. I am personally unreconciled to just about everything.

But all will be well if the creek don't rise.

> Yours every time,
> Eliz.

Korean griddle grease and the smoke from late morning weed in the air, winds light and variable, the sweet-stink of sun-warmed trash bags—this was the Indian Summer the Algonquins had wanted to be rid of, and succeeded, absconding with their jewels and hilarity. The vibrating scorch and scotch of the subway. Sulfurous sewage exhaled from the hard open mouth of the Broadway local. Block after block of brick and concrete buildings—some roaring some asleep—encaged in geometric jungles of scaffolding. Traffic rumbled like a sea, ambulances practiced their glissandos—authority was the merchandise as well as the port. Authority in quotation marks was everybody's brand. Vespas sped by seemingly without riders.

Finn got the young attendant to retrieve the car from the garage—early from the early bird special. While waiting he noted a bicycle rickshaw slowing in front of him. Its driver resembled Pete Seeger, replete with a neat wool cap, a flannel shirt, suspenders. But instead of crooning "Turn, Turn, Turn," he was screaming "Watch! Watch! Watch!" at the top of his lungs. "Watch out for the instructions under the hood! Don't think they're not there! Be afraid of the silver ladies and the pink wires and the shoes the shoes the shoes . . ." The white schizo-phrenics were allowed to ride bikes here. The black schizophren-ics huddled under blankets and cardboard on sidewalks against the façades of the skyscrapers. Pieces of paper rolled into jars with scrawled writing facing outward: *I am not homeless. This is my home.*

"Hey!" The man running the food cart on the corner of Twenty-Eighth shouted at the Pete Seeger bike cabbie. "Dude! You need a burrito!" Then the bike cabbie drove away. The Chel-sea cookware bombs had happened one month before. People were both moving on and not.

The smell of the city in morning, the mix of food and smog, triggered in Finn the trips to strange cities he had taken as a child; he had been made to be up too early, with his school groups, or his family, and now he could feel again the vague terror and strange adventure of a world happening simultane-ously and separately from the world he was from. Cities seemed cobbled together from parts of other cities in other times.

These days people spoke loudly into their own cellphones. He recalled when he had first heard people doing this, at the turn of this century, talking loudly in public on phones he couldn't see. He had been in disbelief. It was like everyone had willingly become insane. The disbelief times were now gone but the voluntary insanity had remained.

He thanked the valet with a ten then headed out. He no longer knew his way around what he called No York: all these neighborhoods telling him "No." "NoHo"—a guffawing denial. "NoMad" where he was staying—of course that was where he was staying. "Nolita." Didn't he date her in high school? Or rather *junior* high? A joke had to be revised, polished, rubbed until the genie got out, ran off, and it just wasn't funny anymore.

His Airbnb was in an industrialized zone of Chelsea and the city jackhammers had kept him up until two in the morning. They were allowed to blast away all night, as if no one actually lived or slept there. He took large swallows of coffee and tested his sanity every morning the same way he did when not on the road: he took out his laptop and replied to the online *Times* editorials, and waited to see if his reply was actually posted. In this manner he could tell, roughly, how deranged he was that day. He had learned to begin with a compliment to the author of the piece. If he started with "Frank Bruni should go back to reviewing restaurants," it disappeared into the ether. But if he began "Frank Bruni is brilliant, yet . . . ," they posted it. Twice he was a Readers' Pick and once an Editors' Pick but mostly he was just part of the pile-on that substituted for breakfast conversation before the comments section eventually closed from inundation. He was "Melvin H from Ohio." And he believed he might be the only Melvin H in Ohio—and since he wasn't really Melvin H from Ohio, he kind of imagined there were no Melvins in Ohio at all. This all was an inefficient way of testing his own mental health and cognition, since he did not believe the online dementia sites. Those online dementia quizzes were gaslighting him!

In the back of his car was his landlady's disposable cat box; before he'd left Navy Lake yesterday morning she had asked him to take it with him and dump it somewhere.

"Really?" Finn had asked.

"Any trash bin will do. Just drive away quickly. I don't know the precise regulations." But Finn had not pulled over. He had driven straight from Illinois, most of the time forgetting the thing was back there, because he always forgot what was back there. But once in a while he heard it. The box slid along the backseat of his Subaru. On a sharp turn it slid to the other side across the seat and banged up against the door.

Driving toward the Bronx was a nightmare but cheaper than a cab. His GPS attempted to redirect him and all was improvisational. The coils of concrete ramps were a mad nest for some giant bird in a horror movie. On the Grand Central Parkway eighteen-wheelers, fulfillment by Amazon, lurked in Finn's blind spot then passed violently on the right, splattering mud on his windshield, which he smeared and smudged and dimmed with the wipers on their frantic high speed as well as the squirters with their buoyant blue spritz. Occasionally a truck let loose with its horn, the salvos of an ocean liner come ashore. He had not approached from this direction in a while and hardly had a moment to ponder the sign for the Triborough Bridge and see how it had become the RFK, a carpetbagging brother bridge to the charming prez's airport. Another thing he could not quite say to his students—for whom he was their official disabuser. But the subject of brothers was on his mind. He was trying to mull moments into anecdotes for his own dying one. They should be anecdotes that were amusing, if the listener were actually leaving this earth. But they should not make the dying laugh in a way that made them want more of life. The dying should laugh wearily in a way that said, *OK. OK. Enough.*

A tough assignment. He was a teacher but didn't really believe in assignments at all, let alone tough ones. Why should anyone have to leave after a day of school only to go home and do more work?

And who *was* Major Deegan anyway?

A take-home exam marked on a bell curve with no liberty, only death. Give me one or the other! Who said that, boys and girls, ladies and gentlemen? And why are these two conditions—liberty and death—considered mutually exclusive? Support your argument with examples.

Finn had been teaching school too long.

Pop quiz (who was your birth father? one out of every ten people have a different dad from the one they think is theirs). Finn himself believed he and Max were only half brothers. How else to explain both the love and the noncomprehension, a pairing that dogged him. Chalk and cheese. This was his own private theory. Their mother had been, well, romantic.

He was approaching the neighborhood of the hospice with a flash of light scarring the periphery of his right eye—from the glare of steel suddenly pulling into view and causing him to veer. The flash was now etched there, another reminder of the proximity of death, as if he needed one more. When he turned his head, it darted and flew like a quick white bat. He supposed much in his life was exactly that: a truck that had not yet hit his vision and so was just lurking blindly there, reaping and grim. The steady crawl of a tsunami in the rearview mirror, coming up from behind. Instead of slowing, he sped up. How scattered their family had become, both brothers figures of displacement, their departed addresses stacking up thinly behind them, as when people once put new postage stamps on top of old ones, in order to reuse the envelope.

He swung onto the first Riverdale exit. In addition to the dried filth of the cat box sliding around behind him, glass shards in a paper bag from a broken goblet rattled farther back in the hatch of his car. He kept forgetting about that—forgot until he took a sharp corner as he was doing now and it all clacked around back there louder than the sliding cat box. The Airbnb had kitchen privileges, and he had voluntarily helped with the dishes, though now he had been asked by his host—in addition to dumping his Navy Lake landlady's litter—to find a replacement amber-hued goblet for the one that had broken when Finn had lifted it, still warm, out of the dishwasher. Tasked onerously by both the Airbnb host and his landlady: this new condition seemed his strange and unexpected fate. Last night Finn had wrapped the glass in a newspaper and placed it in the kitchen trash can. He had failed to leave a note to explain properly. So in the morning the host removed the entirety of it and constructed a tiny sculpture—the stem holding the jagged amber pieces skyward—replete with an angry cardboard sign that read *WTF?* in bright black Sharpie. Because Finn's brother was dying, even the idea of this assignment to find a "replacement glass"—or else he would be fined and kitchen privileges would be revoked, the cardboard also said—irritated the hell out of him. By emptying the dishwasher he had only been trying to help—though he'd been trying to do that his whole life. He had moved out of his Navy Lake condo with Lily so she could have the time to think, which she'd requested, and now he had a landlady's litter box in his car. Then this morning, the note he received alongside the broken glass which included the request "Look at the photos on the crystal sites. Perhaps you will find a replacement online among the special crystal. But you will probably have to look in all the fine glassware shops. I can't remember where I bought it but I absolutely cannot entertain without a matching replacement glass."

Look at the photos on the crystal sites?

Just last month his same Navy Lake landlady had made Finn go to the plumbing showroom to shop for a new toilet to replace the limed-up one his bowels had fallen victim to his second day of residence. The salesman on the showroom floor had sized up Finn's thighs: "You may need a larger seat," he said and had him sit down on several of the toilets in the public showroom. He directed Finn to yet another. And soon Finn was striding from display toilet to display toilet and just sitting on them. "Well now try this higher one? More comfortable for reading? Now stand and face the toilet so we can see how the aim would be."

"I don't think a man has ever spoken so intimately to me before," Finn had said.

And then the salesman showed him how the seat would fall in slow motion rather than with a loud clack. "Your wife will like that." Finn knew he was then supposed to reveal he wasn't married but instead he just said, "Will she?" What he really wanted to say as he sat on various toilets all around the showroom was *May I please have a little privacy?*

He would tell his brother, Max, these stories to amuse and distract him—"It was like taking crap after crap right there in the store!"—to let Max know the madness of the world he was leaving. Not that Max didn't know, but there were illustrations that might ease the transition.

The drive into the hospice parking lot was a concrete descent that seemed endless but purposeful—a preparation for hell. When he found a spot on the final level it seemed like a warm bed for a tired man: all experiences, boys and girls, ladies and gentlemen, express one another if you let them. He got out and locked the door. A fat shimmering purple-necked pigeon, somehow trapped down here, waddled up to him intently like a cat then waddled away.

He had last been with Max during the long months of

chemo but had not until now returned to New York to pay a visit to this hospice. He had been told by Max's wife, Maureen, not to tell Max where he actually was when he asked, or Max would try to leave. "When he asks where he is just say the hospital," she said. Maureen had about two weeks of sobbing that she hadn't gotten around to yet.

"Will you be there?" asked Finn.

"I am so burned out," she said. "You'll see the Ghanaian aide I hired. He's great. His name's William. Sometimes his brother subs for him. They're both very dear."

"William?"

"Yes. William," Maureen said brusquely. "Max will be pleased to see you. If he recognizes you." She exhaled an exhausted unsympathetic sigh: the dying—what a fucking pain in the ass they were.

The elevator up to the lobby and then another one up to the fourth floor were both empty, despite all the cars, as if the parking lot were being used by some other business. One having less to do with death.

He was looking for room 403. He passed through a corridor of photos of Tony Randall, Madeline Kahn, John Lindsay—as if the place were a restaurant and was proud of all the people who had dined there.

Died there.

There was no security stopping him, at a desk, in the hall— what did they need protection from in a place like this? Some visitor who would kill them all with a flu caught on a Carnival cruise? Or some recent retiree who'd spent his pension on stockpiled weapons might burst in and blow them all away? That would be a godsend. And would open up some beds.

At 403 he stood in the doorway. It had been painful—

psychically injurious—to walk through that hallway let alone into a room such as this one. The door—this door of death—was one you passed through and could not turn around and go back out through, whether you were witness or performer. Though of course he and Max would both go back out of it, but only in a bodily way. Everywhere was the smell of alcohol pads, Pine-Sol, and the pesto scent of old urine. He had heard of hospices with views of the sea. This one had a view of a towering brick building across the way. He saw the Ghanaian aide, a mere boy, no older than fifteen surely, sitting in a chair.

"Hey," said Finn.

"Are you Max's brother?"

"Yes," Finn said dumbly, not moving. The hospice gave everyone their own room. Dying was private. But perhaps the mortally ill needed company and should all be together sleeping in the same room. When one person died it was a tragedy. But when two or three people were dying together, it had a chance of becoming a comedy. Not a big chance, but some. Half. Less than half probably.

Fluorescent light rinsed the room. There were a few bent flowers and cards on a side table. Max had not made a particularly good haul for a dying person. Death, where was thy plunder?

The aide's face was cheerful and kind as if eager for any emissary from the outside world, even if it were only Finn. The boy's eyes widened and he pointed to the bed which was hidden to the left behind the door. It seemed to Finn that all rooms should flow to the right, not the left, and that this would be yet another wrong turn. He stepped in to see Max, gaunt with the large sunken eyes of the dying. Max had grown a strange stringy beard, entirely white. What tidings to bring to a man in such shape? Finn had no tidings. Max moved his face slightly to stare at this new visitor, though his eyes goggled around and plastic tubing was taped beneath his nose. The blue cannula of oxygen. Max flicked his long yellowish fingers up in an almost-wave.

"I've come to cheer you up," said Finn.

"Oh," said Max, matter-of-factly, and reached his right hand slowly toward him. "I've become. An object of dismay. I guess." Finn had never seen Max this thin and so had never really noticed the long slender bones of Max's hands, how beautiful they were. Chemo or cancer—who could say?—had eliminated not just the hair on his head but the sprinkle of moles on his neck; his skin was buttery. He had the smooth hue of an apricot. He was a manila envelope getting ready to be mailed. Finn sat down on the edge of the bed. Max closed his eyes and seemed to fall back into the upside-down world of the sick.

"Would you like a chair?" asked the aide, bringing one. What was his name again? William? Finn did not mean to be rude.

"Oh, I'm good thanks—actually, yes, a chair would be nice." He pulled the chair close and sat in it. He would speak to the aide later. Turning his attention to Max, he summoned up the longest sentence he could think of. "Remember how Dad would always begin every conversation with telling you what route he had taken to get there, how there'd been a route he had originally planned to take but how those plans were foiled by construction, and then he'd tell you the routes he used to take back in the day, and how he took this particular outlined route this time, and he would recite all the exits and the highways, along with the weather?"

Max smiled a little. "Do." His stare sometimes fixed itself

pensively into the middle distance, as if he were looking into his own grave. But he had always done that, even as a kid.

"So I'm going to both do that and not do that." Finn reached into the canvas bag he'd brought. He needed props to keep from babbling and props to help him babble. "I brought a photo for you." In it the two of them were holding baseball bats at the local rec field some long-ago year in the '70s. He had put it in a cheap brass frame and now made room for it to stand on the bedside table amidst the plastic tumblers and uneaten applesauce.

"Thanks," said Max, glancing at it. Finn once more noticed Max's silver tooth, arranged by their mother who had been saving money from their cop father's paycheck for her own orthodontia. She had waited twenty-five years for braces on her slightly buck teeth and their father had saved up money. But there was not enough money to keep Max from having a silver tooth his whole life, from when he had chipped it in a fall off his bike and onto the sidewalk when he was nine. It had never been bonded or capped with anything lifelike. He was a forever-pirate on the ship of life and had somehow accepted it. And in the end their mother's orthodontia had straightened her teeth only slightly, her overbite persisting despite all.

"Do you remember this day?" Finn asked, indicating the photo. But why would Max recall? Finn had preserved and re-shaped his memory around this picture, but only he not Max had been in possession of it. So it was all on the new side to Max.

"Sure. Not sure," said Max. His eyes tried to focus. The whites of them were turning the golden earwax brown of bruised fruit.

"Tryouts," said Finn stupidly, and now he would drop the subject. He would sit next to Max and do the harder work. He would say, "Brother, how art thou?" "Don't be afraid." "You were loved." "You were an excellent brother." Would he really say those words, and in the past tense? or just think them but forget to utter each and every one. Since they both had failed at everything else, he would say, "Always know you were a good brother," though he did not even believe in such terms. Good. What is good? Good mother good father good brother good sister. All this usually meant was that you got lucky, that someone had gotten someone into a good college. All it meant was that your zip code was a fortunate one and your metabolism was not bollixed. It did not mean you had found your brother's drug dealer and shot him in the kneecaps. It did not mean you had cured anyone's cancer. Good this. Good that. After years of teaching, Finn did not believe in good anything. He believed in Interesting, Serviceable, Dangerous, Providential, Unlucky, Cruel, Mercurial, Funny, Unreal. He believed time was a strange ocean through which we imagined we were swimming rather than understanding we were being randomly tossed.

"I don't know where I am," said Max. His eyes now were suddenly wide and frightened, darting around the room, terror sometimes passing over his face. He lifted his head but the rest of him did not follow. "I need to get out of here and back into chemo."

Finn could not stick to Maureen's lying, placating script. He would tell Max he was not in a hospital but in a hospice— the place where one dies, when all hope and hospitals are done. The real beginning of the real end. He would tell him the truth.

"You're in the hospital," said Finn, clearing his throat of the lie he had managed anyhow. He was a cooperative coward. "We'll figure this out." There was no one very heroic in their entire ancestral line. He was pretty sure.

Max sank back into his pillow, his eyes swirling in his head. They didn't burn with the last fierce light of the dying but goggled about in their watery way. "I gotta get into chemo," Max said.

Last year when he was in chemo Max would conk out with a Benadryl drip on an easy chair recliner as a plastic bag or toxic brew drained into him through the Hickman port. But not before he would smile and flirt with the nurses who were not even nurses really. "Marry me!" he would say to all the young ones. The meetings with the oncologist that Finn had accompanied Max on were nightmares. The oncologist would sit crosslegged in yoga pants on the examination table and Max would sit in a chair. The doctor would then complain about not having enough research grants from the med school. "So we were all looking for Steve Jobs to help!" the oncologist said more than once. "He could have cured this cancer! His very own cancer! But did he? No, instead he bought a house in Tennessee to be first on the liver transplant list." The oncologist's great brilliance as a healer had been thwarted perhaps by a lack of actual brilliance, and certainly by the unluckiness of his patients, so he would blame Steve Jobs. Why not.

"I'm sure there was money left over," Finn had said nonsensically. "It was just a house in Tennessee."

"You bet there was," said the oncologist. "But it hasn't come to us."

"Yet," said Finn.

The doctor had then closed his eyes. It was easier to speak when you didn't have to look at people. "Max, my friend, you've got about a year. That's when I'm retiring."

But it was now a year and a half later and the oncologist had retired anyway. "I didn't know you'd live this long" had been his lovely departing words to Max, his healer's arms folded, his physician's eyes closed, his pursed mouth suggesting he was partly impressed with Max and with himself and also suppressing a purple shade of shame. He then patted Max on the back and left the room to make contact with his financial adviser and his travel agent.

Now at the hospice the Ghanaian aide came back in with yet another chair.

"I'm Jonathan," said the boy, thrusting his hand out. Finn took it. "I'm William's brother."

"I'm Max's brother," said Finn daftly.

"Yes, I know."

"How old are you?" asked Finn. He was now concerned for the boy. A mere boy in a room of death with adults who didn't know what to do: How could a child know when the adults did not?

"Sixteen."

"Are you too young for this job? It's a heavy job."

"They asked me that when I interviewed. But in my country we see death differently."

Oh, my god, who had told this child to say that?

"We see it as part of life—"

"I'm not dying," piped up Max, who was not asleep after all.

"Yes, it certainly is that," said Finn, completing Jonathan's sentence. Death is the new life, he had started to think. And he hoped it would be cheaper. What if it weren't? What if you got there and they charged for everything? The prices in numbers so long they were a form of computer programming. "Are you watching this TV?" he asked Jonathan. On the screen were two attractive people arguing about someone named Monica.

"Only a little."

"The World Series is on," Finn said. "Please let Max watch the sports channel."

"OK. That's fine. My brother was watching this show before he left and when I took over his shift I just started watching too."

If Finn could get Max watching the World Series, Max would will himself to stay alive until the bitter end. He would watch every game. It wouldn't even matter which team he was rooting for, though if the Cubs could win that would be good. Finn had forgotten of course whether the Cubs had even made it this far. He didn't like baseball the way Max did—more fodder for the half-brother hypothesis. But the nonsense of sports was preferable to most other nonsense.

"I'll be back," said Jonathan, walking backward out the door. Finn glanced up. "The Cubs and the Indians are playing," he said.

"No Cardinals?" asked Max.

"The Cardinals are long gone. Kansas City Royals long gone. But the Cubs are in it. I'm not doing very well cheering you up."

"S'kay. Sgood. Cubs are good. Maureen hates them all. When she's here she's constantly looking at her watch."

"No. No one wears a watch anymore."

"She's looking at her phone."

You have to be actually dead not to see someone looking at their phone, Finn did not say. "What can you do," he said instead.

"How's Lily?"

"Speaking of misery?" Indeed, how *was* Lily? He had never really closed out the tab on Lily. He wasn't over whatever it was they'd had. What had they had? A lot of years. Finn cleared his throat as if it were full of notepads and paper scraps. "I feel demolished every time I see her," he said, sounding lovelorn and ridiculous. "She too is miserable. But since I've moved out to give her space—space she requested in a loud voice, by the way—at long last I don't feel completely responsible for her. And I see her less, so I'm ostensibly more myself, or building back up that way, which may or may not be a good thing. Detach with love, say the lovers of alcoholics."

Let's go to the bar, say the lovers of alcohol.

"How do you know she's miserable?"

Lily had always admired Max. His life is kind of shit, she used to say. Crummy job, iffy marriage, yet he still looks after you. He's still the older brother.

Now looking at Max's face Finn saw nothing but blankness, as if Max were waiting for a bus. It made him briefly homesick for their childhood together: that feeling of being in your flip-flops and swimsuits on a hot asphalt parking lot at the super-market, waiting for your mother to hurry up.

"Well? If you must know the truth?" Finn pulled the chair even closer to Max's bed. "How can I put this: Lily says she wants to die. It's what she always says. I just never told you. This has been her other self. Her secret and mine. But the wishing to die isn't really her. The wish is made into actions and words by her illness. It's an extra room in the house of her head. It's like a spider inside of her telling her from its corner to burn down the whole thing."

"Honey," Lily had once said to him. "You know nothing about mental illness. It's like you should take a course or some-thing." Each of her meds had a generic name and a brand name, long and completely dissimilar to each other like characters in a Russian novel. Her whole condition was one big *Anna Karenina*.

Reciting all this to an actual dying man underscored the absurdity and mystery and mind-boggling waste of someone wanting to do themselves in. It was an obscenity to even think of suicide in a place like this. On the other hand, Finn could see how it might be all you could think of. All things are true, boys and girls. Ladies and gentlemen.

"*Wants* to die?" echoed Max. "Get her in here. We'll show her how. All that wanting's going to wear her out."

"Yeah, and it has kind of devastated me as well," said Finn, and then he remained quiet for a second. "The death watch kind of wore me down. But I'm hanging in there with her. In my fashion. Or rather *her* fashion. I know there's someone else in her life. She thinks she wants to be with him. But I also know, god knows, he can't help her. It can't work. So I'm hanging close." He paused. "Everyone at some point in their lives should have a long great love affair with a magnificent lunatic."

"Yeah," said Max.

Finn squeezed his brother's beautiful hand which was soft perhaps from lotion. Lily's hypothetical death had always been not whether but when, though that is the way with all death. But so many times she had forced him to imagine her dead. All the images he had fashioned—hanging in the garage by a rope, or in the closet by three belts buckled together—all these had deformed his mind.

Max looked away from the television, his eyes wavering in his head, and tried to focus on Finn. "I feel sorry for you, man."

Life's craziness suddenly filled the room like juice to drink. "*You* feel sorry for *me*."

"Yeah," said Max.

The noonday demon, the black downward dog, the devil that had long ago grabbed Lily and rammed her head into the wall. Finn hadn't been deterred. She was beautiful and funny. Sort of. He'd dived. They both would be brave. They would fight illness with love! One had to be a child to be brave. Children were the bravest. And even though now Lily was elsewhere— had left him for someone else fool enough to try (that guy Jack was not going to last; she could always get another less worn-out guy and then wear *him* out)—still Finn thought of her every pathetic day. The prickle and tingle of her was a phantom limb: his mind was independent and self-starting and did not give up in its attempt to enliven the phantom. And even if the limb remained phantom, he knew it was on permanent standby, waiting for a signal. Suspended sensation encircled his head like cartoon stars after a punch.

And yet the deprivation of her intimacy had made a small dent in his heart, and in his breathing, and in the hard candy of his eyes. The thought of her was everywhere but nowhere—an omniscient narrator.

Max breathed deeply. There was another silence between them. Finn knew the visits would continue like this, with long silences to try to absorb the unabsorbable before flicking it away. Or he could work harder to make talk hang in the air like balloons. Batting the words, watching them pop up to the ceiling then float lifelessly down.

"Nobody like Lily," said Max.

Finn smiled. Max still knew all sides of every argument. Lily was mad and maddening, Lily was what-the-fuck. Beautiful as one of those giant apple trees in Russia. Until she started throwing her apples at you, hard hurtful pitches, like the trees in *The Wizard of Oz*. Whenever Finn saw her, she seemed to be in a condition of reverse metamorphosis, turning from tree into woman. Though sometimes she went back again the other way, woman into tree. "If you don't like the fruit, don't come to the orchard," she'd advised him early on. "Too many weird fruits here." Often he felt himself having to bite through the thick fuzzy skin of a peach to get to the apple. She was a magician at leaving him in a state of besotted wretchedness. She was anarchic. "I've banked a lot of chaos," she liked to say. And she had stored it like syrup within her. Whereas other trees had ordinary sap, she had cooked hers into glue for sniffing.

"There, here, on the outer part of your neck are the important meridians. If I press them here can you feel it?" she would say.

He could feel everything.

"See how pressing the meridian pushes pain out and it grows at first but still you can bear it. Its fire burns. But warms. And lights."

"I have a saved message from her on my phone," he said now to Max. " 'Is the weather balmy where you are?' it says. Maybe I'm like the high schoolers I teach, but, man, I think she sounds like she wants to come back to me." Finn grinned as foolishly as possible. He would be a comedy act for Max.

If Finn didn't listen to the message after thirty days it would be wiped clean from the voicemail. He would report in to her when he got back. They had been together too long for him not to. Did it matter to him that she was with another man? This person named Jack? He actually used to like the name Jack but now it was a nail slammed into his temple. Did he have any choice but to go back to her if that's what she wanted? He was unable to love anyone else. He had tried. But always he missed her. He was like a dog, not seeing colors, chasing his own sepia-colored tail, sepia because it was all in the past, one's own tail when chasing it, was in the past, but hey that's where everything he wanted was.

"She still doing the clown thing?" asked Max.

"Yup. I think." Lily did laugh therapy. She dressed as a clown to try to shake people, mostly children, out of their gloom. She understood enfeebling malaise, having so often had her own. And she knew a booming laugh could startle it away. She worked with both children and adults and even wore floppy shoes, the laces of which she had once used to strangle herself.

"I'm sure she's not the only clown who ever attempted suicide," Finn said now. In the end she was all contradiction and felt her life was hers to take—if and when she wanted. "Tears of a clown, boys and girls, ladies and gentlemen."

"Dunno how you manage," said Max. That Finn was suddenly the one to be pitied in this room was a way of making Max feel like the protective older brother again, instead of the sunken dying one, so Finn let it happen.

"To be honest, I don't know either. Don't know how anyone does anything." He would not let his throat constrict and his mouth tighten down again. But his eyes did sting with mist. He took Max's hand and squeezed. "I'm so sorry this is happening to you." Finn's whole head began to weep without a single flicker of movement.

He pulled away for a moment to pluck Kleenex from the nightstand box.

"How's teaching?" asked Max. "Wassnoo? Too cool for school?"

"Ha!" Finn blew his nose. "I'm supposed to be teaching history but I spend part of the time teaching math because no one in that damn high school knows how to teach math." Perhaps he would not tell Max that he'd been suspended for his wanderings away from the curriculum. When in fact he was quite sure it was because he had failed to respond to the headmaster's wife, who was always coming on to him and then in rejection getting irked. Every marriage had a sinister little wobble in it.

"We had good teachers, didn't we," said Max.

"We sure did. We had high-IQ ladies whom feminism later lifted away to med school and law school."

"Oh, well. I don't want to spend my end days arguing with feminism. Really, not the way to sail away to Jesus."

"Now we have parents who are into child promotion and management. They are their kids' own agents."

"Nation of immigrants, man, ever been so."

"I guess. But now even the WASPs are immigrants. Strivers of the worst sort. I guess striving was in the *Mayflower's* DNA."

"Feels strange to be taking all this learning into oblivion," said Max with his eyes closed. Then he opened them and goggled them in Finn's direction. "I look at life and say, what was that all for? What do I do with the times table now? What do I do with my memorized list of presidents and the periodic table and the long recitation, in French, of the kings of France?" His voice was raspy.

"As far as I can see from my students, oblivion's where all learning goes anyway. Sometimes the very next day." There was quiet as they both performed the look of thought about this. Neither made a landfill joke though Finn was trying to find the edges of one and paste it together. Instead he said, "I am taking my own stand against homework."

"Hmmmm?"

Finn would get on his various hobbyhorses and keep talking. "It just measures the home. These students are in school all day! No more! Let them do something else when they go home. Also? I don't read any of their work; it negatively impacts their grade." Finn put his face in his hands. Why next to his brother's deathbed was he going on about school? He fell sorrowfully silent. "Max, my brother, I'm so sorry you're going through this but you have been a trouper throughout and I thought you might win, I really did."

"Jesus, I thought you were here to cheer me up," said Max. He closed his eyes and they both said nothing for a while. "I thought I'd beat it," he said hoarsely. "But death is a fucking genius."

Finn closed his eyes too. "It's certainly an overachiever." Who was anyone but roadkill in the face of it. "Is Cleveland winning?"

"Fucking Cleveland. I thought you said Cleveland didn't make the playoffs." Max closed his eyes again then popped them right back open again and directed his vibrating pain-killed gaze at the television bolted into the ceiling. His eyes were wide with fright. "The Cubs are making a comeback. You watch. They could win. More curveballs than life."

"They could," said Finn, knowing they weren't talking about baseball. "I kind of want Cleveland."

"Oh, come on, no, you want Cleveland? I kind of want Cleveland too."

"Did you know that some players switch the sound of the crowd's cheering in their heads so even when the other team is being cheered they imagine it's for them? This is to manage their own discouragement."

"Ha. S'ats what I'm doing . . . changing the chanting of the crowd."

"Good title for something."

"For my life." Max spoke slowly, changing the subject, in death's drawl. "Snot do mortality. Snot do crazy girlfriends en wives. Let's get back to high school teaching again. . . . Tell me." That was a lot for Max. He breathed deeply except it wasn't deep. The oxygen tubing was slipping on his philtrum beneath his nostrils, and Finn leaned in to straighten it out. Max had to summon such physical strength for each utterance that Finn thought he might accidentally kill his own brother by not holding up his end of the conversation.

So Finn let loose. He believed PowerPoint was bullshit; its dumbing-down of everything was the end of civilization. And there were other concerns: "How can we persuade these kids that what we thought of as a good life was really a good life? How can we persuade them that school, college, work, work, work is what we should be doing? But everyone is buying it." Except Lily, he thought. But Lily was always perverse; she had a trait— gratuitous stubbornness—that he associated with tragedy, with adolescents, with America, with men, with religion. Certain saints had it. Folk heroes. Mysterious women like Antigone or Simone Weil. "Do you realize that not one of my students has ever heard the expression 'the life of Riley'? But why should they? The life of Riley is impossible for them, so it's become a meaningless expression that has quickly bit the dust. And the schools are war zones! Metal detectors at the door! Microaggressions. Trigger warnings and actual triggers! Active shooter drills in kindergarten! Am I sounding entertainingly outraged enough? No one can do math! They all have brain freeze when they get near it as if they had been crushing ice with their teeth. And handwriting is now artisanal!" He was repeating himself. "So I'm teaching them math in History, believe it or not. I devote ten minutes a class period to it and so far no one has reported it or gotten me into trouble and two students have thanked me so there is that."

"History? You doing that?" Max's voice squeaked. Then his eyes closed for a long time and Finn could see him being slowly swept out to sea.

Finn would have to crank it up. He explained how he had become a detective without a trench coat, all suspenseful cluelessness, leading on a retinue of student followers—well, it all looked like an escape from responsibility. He had directed two school plays and invented an elective: The Algebra of Civics; the Civics of Algebra, which he taught along with precalc (no one else knew the material; not one teacher there could divide 54 by 6, at least not quickly). He had been the only one to show private school eleventh graders how to do it. Seven of those teaching years, when he was living with Lily, when they had been together and he had believed in forever and a day, she had teased him about teaching the rich when he hated the rich.

"What are you going to do with all your T-shirts?" Lily had asked.

He, like Max, had ones that read SHARE THE WEALTH and JUMP WITH YOUR FUCKING GOLDEN PARACHUTE.

"They're not all rich" was all he'd said, and he knew personally the three kids who weren't. But he did not hate any of these young privileged children. In fact he admired them a little and enjoyed them a lot and they filled him in on their world as if they themselves were spies in their own lives and just as astonished as he was, the parties at Rockefeller Center, the entire ice rink rented out, the trips to Tahoe or Taos. But he hated their parents, whose inner lives had only half-formed before stiffening and going still. And he hated the world they grew up in. When he passed back the tests the students quickly took pictures of their grades with their cellphones and sent them to their eager mothers.

"I'm doing Counter-History," he explained to his dying brother. "I'm doing Alt-Consensus History and things I don't precisely call conspiracy theories—but I'm trying to reclaim the term *conspiracy theory.* Taking back the night. Taking it back from the barbarians. People talk about 'conspiracy theories'— Pizzagate and bullshit like that. Those aren't conspiracy theories. Those are psychotic mirages. A conspiracy means more than one person plotted together and hello, you bet your ass they did. But if you discredit the term then you're left with nada. A theory means a hypothesis has been tested. That is, it's put through the car wash of some research. I'm not talking about deranged political hallucination. I'm saying, Kids? Probably more than one crazed guy was in on this. Society pulls the trigger. The lone gunman theory offends our common sense. I let them sit with all their feelings and disagreements. I give them their rhetorical safe spaces because this is the school shooting generation, and they don't have actual safe spaces, not even movie theaters, so they need rhetorical ones, extra courtesies, new gentle and acknowledging terms. But I traffic a little in 'conspiracy theories' as *we* used to understand them, ones that put groups and systems back into the situations where individuals were taking the rap. I'm not a denier of any tragedy, just skeptical about the cleanup crew. I want to bring questioning all Official Versions back to the Progressives. The moon landing in 1969 or the ostensible search for and capture of assassins or whatever needs a squint. I'm in the 'doesn't that sound fishy' school of fish. Ritual burials at sea? Really? I say, 'Boys and girls, what are some reasons that an inexplicable event at Roswell might have been kept as a government secret? Sixty percent of Russians think America did not land on the moon. No one in Eastern Europe thought we did. They thought it was just Cold War bullshit.' "

"Yeesh, yer not fired yet?" said Max.

"I split the difference and say we did land on the moon, but perhaps later, not in 1969, which could very well have been enacted bogus stuff, JFK's schedule honored. Cold War pageantry. 'Who benefits, boys and girls? Why did the Apollo program cease and desist as soon as the Soviets had deep space technology?' "

"You trying to shock me back to health? Ya telling them your theory that syphilis wrote the Constitution? I remember once when you were saying that."

"Yeah, that was last year. But listen: As soon as women started becoming astronauts, why did we stop landing on the moon?"

"Why?"

"Because women would not have kept their mouths shut about this! Still not a single woman has landed on the moon!"

"I get you." Max winked. "Sort of."

"Why did NASA send memos in December 1968 saying *Help! We cannot make this tight political schedule! Apollo 1* had blown up right on the launchpad the year before."

"Hmmph."

"As for the ostensible lone assassins? I say to my students, What are some reasons do you think that James Earl Jones got all the way to Canada and then to London, where he robbed a bank and a jewelry store when money he was waiting for didn't arrive, and then got to Portugal; how was it that this assassin was on the lam for sixty-five days? Sponsored by somebody? You bet. The King family themselves don't believe a word the FBI ever said on the matter. And the man on the Lorraine Motel balcony, holding King's head with a towel? A CIA plant. And the man taking the picture? An FBI one.' "

"Ray. James Earl Ray. Not Jones."

"That was a test! Wow. Man, you are so not going to die. I'm the one who is going to die. In fact, shove over, I'm lying down next to you."

"Can't move."

"Never say never." Max's body consisted of long bones inside saggily draped, blue-webbed skin. Sinewy as a week-old fryer chicken.

"Din say never."

Finn got up and slid in on his side against the metal bed rail and put his head next to Max's and began to whisper. "It's like all the things we talked about as kids. *You* told me this one: The real story is never the official one. So we must imagine skeptically around the corners and over the walls. So with the students? I do history's hot spots and repetitions. Then I do math as refreshment." He paused. "Which is how I figured out that I could fit into this bed here. I did some fast mental work with parallelograms."

"Math's OK. I like history." There was no saliva in Max's mouth. Just the odor of an old mimeograph.

"You got to teach kids that if it adds up too neatly it probably isn't correct."

"Is that the math part? Or the history. Be careful. You'll hear from HR."

"For an event to be real it has to have that strange imperfection and contradiction that gives it reality. Eliminating the groups, the conspirators, you don't have reality anymore, you have something neat that you can control. Without understanding the underlying thinking of the group, what we are told is incomplete and feels unsatisfying. What are some reasons do you think that John Wilkes Booth got around so easily—New York, Montreal—and was also on the lam for quite a while, eleven days—or years some say—and his body may have been misidentified and never precisely found, officially buried three times but perhaps unofficially never, and not returned to the family, some of whom believed he was still alive and made it all the way to Bombay. The Union did acknowledge a fake burial of him in the Potomac plus an additional one a year later, though through the decades there were dozens of ostensible sightings. But they needed a story that could bring the drama to a close. They needed mad Boston Corbett in a blazing shoot-out to 'kill him' and then go further mad and disappear entirely. No one knows what happened to Boston Corbett."

"Really?"

"The Jack Ruby of the nineteenth century! Why did people say they saw both Booth and Corbett out west all the way into 1905 or whatever? So I say to the kids, 'Boys and girls, ladies and gentlemen, how do all the unlikely but official versions of these events actually ease and simplify matters for the people in power? JFK? A nut is simpler than a mafia hit. MLK? A nut is simpler than a KKK hit. Lincoln? A nut is simpler than a network of Confederate spies and double agents in the federal government. Well, of course they all conveniently work with nuts. And take a squint at Stanton! A team of rivals—you bet, boys and girls, ladies and gentlemen. And don't forget poor Abe's bodyguard who left the theater box unguarded in order to go get a beer and then *he* disappeared forever. Why of all the four people hung for the assassination did not a one of them actually kill anyone? The rich always triumph over the poor and manage to avoid the cost of wars begun by them. Begun by the rich, I mean. Plantation owners escaped conscription while the poor fought in their stead for the right to own another person they themselves could never afford.' A teacher is supposed to get kids to think critically. As in this: What happened to the missing eighteen pages of Booth's diary when it was finally, belatedly produced by Stanton?"

Finn, from his various hobbyhorses, attempting to engage his brother, could feel himself getting carried away. He felt mad as a hatter, in the way that facts no one else believed in could make you feel. His ongoing rehabilitation of the term *conspiracy theory* was a lonely walk in the desert. He now added, "Courtesy of Lafayette Baker, who appears later to have been poisoned." Finn wiped beads of sweat from his own brow.

"You sure can talk. But I have a question," Max said softly, raising his hand a little. "When there's lots already for these kids to learn, why would you add all this to the pile? You're worrying me."

"I'm not adding to the pile. I'm subtracting from the pile." But he told Max that he was questioning even Democracy—which, though a fine idea, the country had never actually had. It was just performative, a little parade down Main Street.

And that was when Finn told him he'd been given a leave

of absence from his school. He'd been suspended due to a lot of personal matters that included rebuffed advances from the headmaster's wife, Sigrid, whose feelings he had wounded when he would not take her up on various lustful suggestions and requests. He was doomed to retaliation either way in that situation. A suspension he could handle. What was there not to handle, ten weeks' paid leave. A time out. A little humiliation. Fuck it.

"That sucks." Max exhaled his carbon copy of a breath, and his eyes searched the television for a score and an inning. "Be careful, man. The students will question authority all right. They'll question yours. They'll think critically about *you,* and *you'll* find yourself with some missing pages as well." The exhaustion it took to speak. Speaking was simultaneously under- and overrated. "You might never get your job back. Also?" Max added. "Don't let the nurses hear you. I like to get extra snacks. You're gonna scare them away."

Finn kissed Max on the forehead. "As I said, the school has no one else in that building who can teach math. So they need me. I'll be back. Do you want anything? How about a little water?"

"Mmm."

Max stared at the ceiling so much that Finn said, "I'm going to get you some pictures of naked women and tape them up there. But right now I'm getting you hydrated." Finn got up and went out into the hall searching for a cooler. Or a beverage machine. He wasn't going to use the filthy taps anywhere in this town. Perhaps he had become a bona fide paranoid.

He walked quickly down the hall, alone, looking, looking for water. Lily behind his eyes saying, "Ask." Lily's force field: a reposeful explosion of nature. There she was, always with him though he would like to bat her away. He rubbed his brow as if his head ached though he was simply trying to knead her out of his thoughts.

He looked for a nurse. But perhaps it was too close to lunchtime to find one, an early afternoon lull, perfect for invisibility. He had once as a young man taken a professional aptitude test which concluded that he should be either an orchestra conductor or a nurse. Now he couldn't even find a nurse let alone be one. He had always liked to conduct the radio, however, and perhaps if he started to do that now in front of the speakers in the lobby some nurses would quickly appear. Destinies could merge. He was tempted. He had once taken online a mental wellness challenge, in which every third question transparently attempted to set a trap. (1) Sometimes I feel sad and find that walking helps. Yes. (2) Talking to people I like boosts my mood. Yes. (3) Sometimes I can fly around the room but I keep this a secret from others.

"Nurse?"

A wide ruddy brunette in a white uniform was walking toward him.

"Can we get a little juice or something in here?"

"Surely."

"Also, while I have you here. I just want to say. Max has got great insurance. You don't need to move him along, if you know what I mean."

"No, I don't know what you mean," she lied.

"He's grandfathered in for that state employee's clause for Unlimited Hospice. Or something to that effect. No need to hurry him. No cap on the stay. You'll be paid handsomely for every single day." Did it sound too much like a rhyme to sound true? But it was true.

The nurse said nothing but went into another room where Finn could see there was a refrigerator and a counter. And there the nurse poured juice. Which wasn't actually real juice but a bright red drink of some sort. Perhaps Gatorade. Perhaps methadone. If the methadone here didn't kill you, the other beverages might.

Suddenly Max appeared at his side. "I'm glad you're mentioning that but it probably is all for naught."

"You're ambulatory? What the fuck?"

Finn briefly turned back to see the nurse approaching with the bright red drink.

"We don't manage the beds," she said. "Besides, which Max do you mean?"

"The Max right here . . ." Finn said. But he saw that his brother was no longer there. "The Max down there," he said, pointing toward Max's room. This was what happened when you traveled around with a litter box in your car.

She started to bring the beverage herself but Finn said, "I'll take it in."

"Fine," she said. "No problem."

He walked back to the room with a plastic cup of the red Kool-Aid. Max was completely in bed, taped up with the oxygen flow to his nose. Beneath the sheet there was a diaper holding soaked urine close to the bedsores. It seemed no way to live and no way to die. Was this the best civilization had to offer right now? It was like one long committee meeting in this place.

"This is what she gave me," he said to Max. "Unless you'd prefer to start with white."

"I never start with white," said Max.

"I sort of remember that," said Finn. "Is there another Max on this hall?"

"Yep, I think so."

"Does he look like you?'

Max just stared at Finn, and then his eyes started goggling again.

"They were talking about him out there. Don't let them get you guys confused. I'm sure you've got the better insurance."

Max's eyes closed—he was being slowly pulled out to sea again—but he fought it and his eyes opened, focused, a slight flash of blood to his face. Death was a sea and Life was another sea.

Approaching the end was like light coming back from a dead star—a trick. But Finn knew the red stars were the dying ones and strangely the blue ones were hot and new. And Max's eyes were blue. "'Member when Mom used to take the other Max's craft projects?"

Finn remembered now Max telling him this once. That their mother on Parents' Night at school, when they lined up all the kids' clay ashtrays and flowerpots with their first names written on the bottom, had taken the other Max's art project. The other Max was a better artist and made better bowls so she would take the other Max's stuff.

"She used that other Max's ashtray for years."

"Did her in."

"Yup. Death by other Max. She should not have loved that other Max's work so much."

Finn thought in agreement: Yes, if she'd taken home her own son's ugly crenellated fingerprinted one she would have quit smoking for sure. Regrettable things kept accruing in life until it was done and you got to say, Well that's over. Or didn't get to say, That's over. But someone was there to say it for you if need be. On the other hand, he knew, memories were often tampered with before they were put back on their shelves. Stories, told enough times, replaced the memories which, once uttered, dissipated and remodeled themselves. It happened at a cellular level: everyone was narratively rewritten. Perhaps their own heavyset, black-haired mother was the sweetest and most attentive in the world. But no one asked for that book at the library. And so perhaps it was sold in some benefit sidewalk sale or just morphed into the story she was for her sons now: Someone who took in too many foster daughters. Someone who smoked too much. Someone who wished she'd had girls. Who could blame her. The girls she'd taken under her wing were impressive—though he had lost touch with all of them. Perhaps the social imperatives of living had always been obscure to their entire family. The foster sisters had generated their own wings and had used those wings to fly away from their mother and the entire household really.

But their mother was not so bad. She had wanted those girls to have a mother. She was the only person in any of their lives to really try. And on her deathbed their mother, paralyzed by tumor-induced stroke, looked beautiful and brave and gave Finn a wink that let him know she was in on everything.

"Does she attempt it?"

"Who, what?"

"Lily. Take her own life."

"What can I tell you." What could he? "I have been her suicide hotline for some years now," Finn said.

"Oh, geez."

Finn hesitantly told Max about Lily's hospitalization the previous year, where stripped of all means of injuring herself, no jewelry, no soap, no sash, ties yanked and tossed from the sweatpants and the hoodies, she had entered the shower, nude, possessed of nothing but several moments of determination, and held her face up to the water to drown herself. She was given her privacy. The water had streamed into her sinuses and lungs. No one knew. But when too much time had passed someone stepped in and at the last minute she was dragged out by an aide, water was pressed out of her, and an ambulance took her to intensive care. And she had lived. "Not really living," she had said.

"Yes, it is, damn it," Finn had said, wanting to shake her. "This is life! It's not fucking perfect. It's not even all that great. But it is the only living part you've got and yes it's a mixed bag!" He understood that suicide was a mystery and not answerable by anything he might think or say. It was an opera about trying to escape. And although all operas were about trying to escape, in real life operas had curtain calls. The suicide in opera was followed by rising up and taking a bow, by resurrection and applause.

Max reached over with his golden hand and laid it on top of Finn's. Finn felt the stabbing sting of sorrow in his own eyes, as if all the world were moving away from him.

"Feel sorry for you, man," said Max and he really seemed to—how the fuck was that possible? How was his dying-in-agony brother again feeling sorry for *him*?

"Let Lily die," said Max. "Or not," he added, closing his eyes. He shifted uncomfortably. "I know: The heart wants the shit that it wants . . . Ow . . . fucking catheter's a bitch. Anyway." He breathed with difficulty. "Prolly snot up to you."

"Maybe not." Finn was pathetically, pathologically drawn to Lily's richly bleak disposition. Perhaps because heterosexuality in general was looking a little doomed he embraced the doom, the hormonal override of common sense. It seemed amazing, given everything, that men and women could love one another in any way whatsoever. So when it was managed—when it existed here and there in all its precariousness—was that not a beautiful bit of ruin? Everyone was always a little maddened by love because love was either hesitant or overpowering. It was never properly calibrated. It was an aggravation. It was not meticulously directed, which is perhaps why she had strayed.

Max just needed Finn to talk. Finn could see that. So he continued to fill the air with whatever popped into his head.

"I blame her medications. She was feeling blue and the doctors began to chase that blue feeling with all these crazy prescriptions, one on top of another, polypharmaceuticism or some such obscuring term for malpractice. The pharmaceutical industry, see, sends the shrinks on promotional tours, gives them free pills and free pill cutters and calendars and coffee mugs and matches and lighters and ashtrays—did you know they still give out lighters and ashtrays? It's a crime and a racket."

Max breathed in wordlessly, effortfully. Sickness detached a person from the world and at the end shrank that world down to the size of a room, the walls of which vibrated and stepped slowly, slowly forward.

When the World Series came back on, Finn would watch with him. Cleveland was ahead. It was a nice break from the election. The whole year was becoming one big fuck-you year: politicians to their parties, voters to the candidates, candidates back to the people, Stockholm to novelists, Bob Dylan to Stockholm. All that was left was the Cubs and the Indians.

"Those pills hardly did anything to help her but then she couldn't get off them without major repercussions. It was as if she had moved into a strange little village that would neither feed her nor let her leave. And she was never right after that. Every neuron had some chemical thimble over it and where her brain was once a lively orchestra of notes it became this dour little string quartet. Sawing away with Beethoven's dark deafness but with little else resembling Beethoven . . ."

Max closed his eyes. He moaned a little, twisting his body with a slight wince. He no doubt had bedsores all up and down, and the staff did not adjust for them since what the hell, bedsores were the least of it. The staff was a life force! And life moved you through it like a conveyor belt. The whole Enterprise of Life was snooty and didn't really want that much to do with death. Death made Life look bad. Finn should go back to the subject of the moon landings, how the first one suspiciously went off without a hitch while the others, the ones that were real, all had issues. Of course Max would think this was how Finn got suspended from his job. Max would think the stuff about the headmaster's wife, Sigrid, was more bullshit than the first moon landing.

"Brother, where art thou?"

"Still here."

"Can I help you get comfortable?"

Max said nothing. His eyes were open and swimming around.

"I'm staying here to watch the Series with you. It'll perk you up." He had not asked after the kids. "I neglected to ask after the baby. How old is she now, two?"

"Three."

"Three! She must be talking up a storm."

"Yeah." Max heaved a sigh. "But a lot of what she says is total crap."

Finn laughed. *I miss you already, man,* he did not say.

Who would be at Max's funeral? Funerals now were a cross between Christmas and death, relatives hugging, smiling not always through tears, telling funny stories. Funny! But for his older brother Finn imagined merely an empty chapel. Max had seldom attended church and the death part would lack the Christmas part. Maureen would sit in the back row, holding the three-year-old. The only other children would be a boy from her previous marriage and perhaps some little friends of the officiating priest.

"I do kind of want Cleveland," said Max after his wincing was over.

"They're scrappy," said Finn. "They want it. Plus they've got Carlos Santana on their team."

"Didn't know he could play . . . ball."

"No one did! It's a miracle, that much talent bundled together."

"Swhat I missed in life: talent bundled together."

"Hey, you're good at a lot of things. You were good even at baseball."

"Life was good at it. Curveballs."

"Yeah," said Finn, "baseball is really the game that tells you what life is going to be: fastballs, errors, wild pitching, clutch hits, strike-outs, not getting to first base, things coming in from left field. Near misses. And that's just the romance part." He followed Max's wordless gaze. "Rizzo's foot is off the bag—Cleveland should challenge it."

"Yeah."

"I think calling them Indians is a microaggression against Native people and that's why I have to root for the Cubs."

Max stared at the TV. Finn could see Max was rooting for both teams. He was rooting for both teams to go on forever so he wouldn't die. "Why aren't they challenging it?"

"A near miss. Shouldn't it be called a near hit?"

"No, it can't be a hit of any sort. It's not a hit. But it's close. So it's a miss."

"Which has come near. Near misses are a problem. By the way, don't let anyone switch the channel to some stupid movie," said Finn. "Look at that. Arrieta's itching to pitch."

The sun was sinking, sending its thin horizontal light through the windows, even though the clocks had not yet been set back.

"By the way," said Finn. "Who the hell was Major Deegan?"

Max suddenly seemed to be able to focus and his face collected itself into an expression of beautiful blankness. "Major Deegan? Jesus, Finn. I'm dying here. Did you bring any weed?"

"I'll get you some," Finn whispered.

"I mean for you," Max said, and attempted to smack Finn's arm with a floppy hand, but his long fingers just lifted and fell. He brought the back of his hand up to one eye. "My eyes are all scratchy. I'm dehydrated I guess."

"Here, drink this maraschino juice," said Finn, bringing the plastic cup of it to Max's lips. "It'll stain your lips and make you look like a drag queen."

Max waved it away.

"Or here." Finn pulled a small bottle of artificial tears from his pocket. His ophthalmologist had prescribed it. "My dry-eye lady recommends this. Chin up and look back." Max cooperated for a change and Finn squeezed a drop into each of his eyes.

"Your dry-eye lady?" Max said afterward. "Y'gotta dry-eye lady?"

"It's like a blues song, man. Why not."

Then they both began to sing: "Got a dry-eye lady," sang Max.

"Knows how to wet my eye."

"Got a dry-eye lady."

"She always makes me cry."

Max closed his eyes, no longer in the song. "Miss you, man," said Finn. He took Max's hand. He didn't squeeze it since Max would not be able to squeeze back.

"Miss you too," Max said, which seemed an admission that he wasn't going back into chemo. Finn knew Max's immune system was shot. And that even when it was going strong an immune system was not organized, it was very ad hoc, without choreography. Currently, it was a bunch of street dancers lying in the park pretending not to know one another.

"Were there things we should have done as brothers that we didn't do?"

"It'll be OK," said Max.

"Things we should have said?" Perhaps Finn was becoming embarrassing. "Did we say them?"

"Yeah, mostly. Man, there's a ball game here."

Soon a different nurse came in and closed the shades. Innings went by with howls and affirmations and long, long pauses, and soon game three of the Series was done for the night. Max was asleep.

Finn went down to the parking lot to look for his car. Looking for his car in a parking lot was such a familiar event that it had become a recurrent anxiety dream. Where was his car? He would not have a clue but time was of the essence. And then a metanarrator of the dream would step in and say, "Don't be anxious: This is just a dream. You don't need to find any car. This is a problem you don't have to solve. This is just a dream."

And his stubborn, still asleep self always said back to the narrator, "But wouldn't it be a good idea to find the car anyway? Wouldn't it be a good mental exercise to actually locate it in this lot?"

And the metanarrator said, "This is a dream. A dream does not contain an actual parking lot."

And Finn asked, "Is the car an actual car?" and then always woke up, anxiety still rumbling around inside him.

But this here was real life and despite the dreams he was unprepared.

On the way back to his Airbnb, Finn couldn't recall who had won that day's Series game.

The next morning after he bought a Cleveland Indians cap at a corner gift shop, he drove straight up the Avenue of the Americas, then swung over on Fifty-Sixth. Trump Tower was crowded with NYPD, once upon a time his father's own employer— Courteous, Professional, Reliable was their CPR, to pretend to help you breathe—who could breathe? We can't breathe! No one can breathe!—and Finn parked his car near a Commercial Parking Only sign, round the corner from Gucci, and left his blinkers on. Soon there would be bomb-sniffing dogs, a true Checkpoint Charlie, but right now there were no dogs at all, because Trump was eventually going to lose, so until then just cops and steel crowd gates like bike racks. He looked up at the building's statuary—a scantily clothed man holding up a clock—was that not everyone he knew? He walked quickly into Tiffany's with his bag of broken goblet and showed it to the greeter at the door, who was a young man wearing a boy's tight-fitting suit, this new style that caused grown men to look like they were fourteen-year-olds outgrowing their clothes. Finn guessed that was the point. The greeter by the door also wore a light blue wool scarf hanging from his neck. "Crystal's on the fourth floor," said the man, pointing at the elevator. "Someone there might be able to help you." The whole main floor looked austere and strangely futuristic and bare, as if it had already been robbed. Finn waited at the elevator but it seemed too slow. So he took the stairs. Twenty-one flights to the fourth floor—those were some high ceilings. He was out of breath. More men in too-small suits and light blue scarves awaited him. This winter accessorizing in October seemed to suggest they were already anticipating a blue Christmas in honor of the election, although every Christmas was a blue one at Tiffany's.

"May I help you?"

"I'm hoping so," said Finn. "I'm afraid I've broken this valuable goblet and I can't find any place that carries this line for a replacement. So I thought you might have it or would know someone who did."

The man peered into Finn's bag while holding it open. He then reached in and pulled out a piece. "Hmmmmm . . ." he said. He held it up to the light. He then summoned another salesclerk. "Zig? Does this ring a bell to you?"

Zig moved quickly in his too-small suit. He looked at the shard and made a face.

"We never carried that," he said.

"Do you know a place that might have?"

"Honestly? I have a couple of these. They were on sale three years ago at Pottery Barn."

The glass shard was dropped back into the bag. "Thank you," said Finn. He would save these shards to stick them in his Airbnb host's tires. Or just take them back and spell out POTTERY BARN with the little pieces.

At the Bronx hospice his brother was asleep; an orange Popsicle melted on his chest, an untouched plastic bottle of Ensure on the table. Death was sending mixed messages. Finn picked the Popsicle up and put it in the bile-hued plastic bowl by the bed. He found some Kleenex and dabbed at the corners of Max's mouth and wiped his chest. He placed the navy and red Cleveland hat on him, sideways, jaunty. Max still didn't wake up. William smiled from his chair, looking up from his soap opera.

"Can we keep this on Sports News?" Finn asked again.

"I'm very sorry. Your brother fell asleep so I thought I'd watch . . ."

Finn already liked Jonathan better than William.

"He'll always tune out unless you keep it on the sports station. Let him rewatch the plays from the previous night's game. He'll stay alive as long as Cleveland manages to stay in it. Let me prove it to you." He took the remote and turned to Sports News, where some clips from earlier Indians games were being aired. Sure enough, Max opened his eyes and stared out from beneath his cap.

"It's just as well I'm dying," he said during the commercial. "I don't want to be around for Donald Trump being president."

"Never going to happen."

"Trump said the thing he dislikes most about himself is his hair. Women are going to vote for him."

"To have a president so off script can never happen. He wanders so far off he seems to just step off the planet, as if the world were flat and one could do that. Don't check out of this life thinking Trump's going to be president. Don't go with that hallucination or *I* will *really* feel sorry for *you.*" With the election worries his brother was sinking into the underground caves of delirium. "Leave thinking Cleveland will win. Or better yet don't leave at all," Finn croaked. When his parents had died his chance to be their wonderful child was finished—so close yet so far: What was the meaning of that failed proximity? With his brother would it be the same in terms of brotherhood? Here Max was so lingeringly close to the end that maybe the end would never quite arrive, and instead they might grow their brotherhood like a beautiful garden at long last though of course it would be a puny garden since they had waited too long to get it properly and clearly planted.

Finn's phone beeped and low-level dread burst into his pounding heart. Once it had been Lily he worried over. Then Max. Now both. These were the children he worried about. People are often happier without children, he once said to a class for no reason at all.

A text on Finn's phone flashed: *Please call me.*

It was from Sigrid, who in addition to spoiling his life a little was one of Lily's book group compatriots. He wrote back: *I'm in NY with my brother. What's up?*

Re Lily.

What about? She take off?

Come home was the reply.

I've got a cat box and a bag of broken glass in my car, plus a mortally ill brother. I can't just come home.

You must come. It's Lily. Our book group meets tomorrow. But I will cancel or winnow it down. Please come. Urgent matters.

He took out his checkbook and wrote William a check for $1,000.

William grinned. "Want to see my signature? This is how we endorse checks in our country." And he wrote *William* on the back with twelve m's then counted them aloud to make sure there were in fact twelve. Then he added his last name.

"Don't lose that," said Finn. William put the check in his pocket.

"Never do," he said.

Finn leaned into Max's ear and whispered, "I have to return to Navy Lake, but I'll be back here as soon as I can. We haven't finished all our conversations. I still have some things I want to tell you." He paused. "And I don't mean 'You can let go now.' I'm never going to tell you that." Who was anyone to tell a person that? "So I need you to not let go. I need you to hang in there, watch the Series, I'll be back. I'm your death doula, bro." He knew people were often quite accidentally not with family members when they died. They were out taking a brief walk. Or getting a bad snack in the awful cafeteria. Then they come back upstairs and the beloved had passed. He would try to get lucky and not have this happen.

"Don't get fired, man," whispered Max hoarsely.

"Failure is a form of vacation," said Finn. "Or at least usually involves one."

Then he left the bardo of the hospice to its trapped souls

and the steel beds and alarmingly colored drinks. He knew the average number of days in hospice care was seventeen and that most people died after three. But he left Max and headed for the elevator with an illogical sense of hope. Max would have to wait to die and Max, Finn felt sure, would do his best to wait. In a way, Finn thought foolishly, he was handing Max extra time.

He went back to the NoMad Airbnb and folded up the towels he'd used and left them at the foot of the bed. The landlady came to the doorway and pulled on one of the towels, one with a rip. "Oh, my, did I give you this towel? I didn't meant to do that. That's the dog's towel."

"Doesn't matter now," said Finn. "There's an emergency and I have to leave early. You can keep the change." He handed her the bag of broken glass and said, "This is from Pottery Barn."

She did not say anything, as if she already knew.

"I will send you a new set as similar as I can find," he added insincerely, for he knew they were a clearance item.

He grabbed his packed bag and located his car, then drove downtown, still with the cat box, through the Holland Tunnel into Jersey then hours along scored and flattened ribbons of interstate marked with signs for Hardee's and British Petroleum (this in exchange for support of the Iraq war, he had told his students! Though he wasn't sure about that one).

All the rush hours were long behind him, so he could rush alone, the autumn sun stretching across the hills. Warehouses and outbuildings seemed to gain on him in his peripheral vision, like merging traffic, and he pressed his foot to the gas to pull ahead of them. He would drive straight back home, bird-brained, as the crow flies. He would make the seventeen hours through the keystone, the buckeye, then whatever a hoosier was to the sweet land of Lincoln. Or, rather, the land of sweet Lincoln. When he talked about Lincoln to his students, tears bit at his own eyes. He once had read Lincoln's letters aloud to his students. Despite the downward slope of the handwriting (he would make photocopies and pass them out) they had a brilliant lightness to their heavy heart. He found himself choking up. Oh, boys and girls, ladies and gentlemen, if only he had gone to see *Aladdin* that Good Friday evening, which is what he had wanted. But you can't put the genie back in the bottle. Sometimes when Finn looked at a five-dollar bill he just had to put it away. Perhaps he was too emotional to pay in cash, or to teach history. Which was why, when he taught math to these kids who weren't being taught math very well elsewhere, he could feel composed.

Now he was in the Pennsylvania part of Appalachia, running between the tight shale walls, the highway snaking round every mountain. The brown brush of the prewinter hillside like a wide-bristled doormat, reminding him that he had not shaved.

The roads were becoming slick with a glaze of ice then wet with water as the temperature moved between 31 and 33, solid and liquid. A symbol of changing matter! Was he paying attention to symbolism? Why not. Soon again he was passing by quite a few Homewood Suites with their kitchenettes, and Country Kitchens with their month-old chicken pieces under lights.

Speeding off into the dusk, away from the muddying urban light soon into the clarity of white stars against black, he fiddled with the radio but reception wasn't good. He had let his satellite radio subscription lapse. So he made due with singing "Moon River," where his own name implied in the lyrics had been replaced with "friend." OK. He would be everybody's friend. In a Huckleberry way.

Life felt less short when driving back home felt this long.

Somewhere ahead and above him in the terrible spitfire of the stars was Orion or Perseus or the Chicago Bears. Who knew. He could never pick out Orion or Perseus. Or any of the constellations from the random clusters and throngs and doilies. He assumed others were not actually pretending when they said they could—*don't you see?* He had never been good at connecting dots—sad fact but most facts were. He had lain there on blankets in fields his whole boyhood completely baffled. It seemed you needed to be a radiologist to read the sky. Smashed glass strewn across the night: bone chips and eddies of pneumonia. The mythic figures seemed like nonsense—somebody's desire to fill vast sparkly terrifying emptiness with ancient heroes assembled from the whimsical lines of an inscrutable woodcut. Was that an arm? Was that a buckle? The Dog Star. Was that even a thing? Did it have a leash and become confused with the Big Dipper, a kitchen item no one even used anymore? Maybe Taurus was really Merrill Lynch. Perhaps Orion was an Irish bartender who could whip up drinks with the flash of his belt, keeping Aquarius in his unbearable cups. Celestial jokes! Everything was just wheeling glitter tossed on a coat.

But ah the moon, he felt, when he could see it, moving as it did through clouds and the clouds through it, had substance. It had a gibbous side that healed itself. Never showing you its dark side. Never asking you to see the pocks as anything but pocks. You did not have to try to see the old man's face looking down if you didn't want to; and if you wanted there it was, without trying, its Edvard Munch–like O of a mouth. Occasionally you could see it shining in a river on a still, still night.

Where was Lily? Over and over his calls went straight to voicemail.

She had slipped away, and now this unexplained summons clanged like a bell. Whenever he thought of her lately it was in photographs. The photos of them together—smiling, entwined, behatted, insouciant—were like all photos: weak lies at the time but full of truth and power later on. A weird form of time travel.

Now smoky fog gathered in the little valleys of the road and sleet spangled the windshield, including the murky semicircles of darkness his wipers tried to create, first slowly then frantically when he turned them on high. Snow flurries began to show up in his high beams, blowing down at an angle, swirling then disappearing in the road. A Doppler shift. He stayed in the passing lane moving at the speed of fright. Ha! But then headlights came behind him in the dusk, catching his far side mirror, and a car began to pass him on the right, and when he slowed down his own car began a slippery drift toward the passing one. *The car is my shepherd I shall not want. It makes me.* In order not to hit the car to the right he steered a little left and then he was sliding full speed off the road. His car spun and everything slowed, or the perception of everything slowed, the way it does when your body is giving you time to save yourself, the way the pitcher's ball is slowed by the mind so that the batter can actually detect and hit it, if he can. The car spun twice, and everything went into slow motion to give him time to save his life, but he had no idea what to do with this time, how to pull out of this skid, and branches and water and shrubs were suddenly thrust and flattened against his windshield, as if he were going through a car wash. The windshield had become a mad expressionist painting—a mosaic whose tesserae were seceding from the Union. Pieces of swarming night nature pressed against the sides and the hood, as if peering in, then moved away.

His car landed in a field facing back in the direction he'd come from, wheels stopped dead in the wet snow and mud and the engine cut dead. He suspected he was in Ohio. When not paying attention in life he assumed you could end up in Ohio. The car had lost all life but nothing seemed smashed. He seemed to have bumped his head against the door window but no airbags had been triggered. He wiped his brow and felt a smudge of blood. He had been in a car accident only once before in his life when his cop father had spun off the New York Thruway, also in snow, with the entire family inside. Everyone had broken one bone.

Now he opened his driver's side door and got out. He could try to open the hood and look inside but he knew he would have no idea what he was looking at. He took his phone out of his jacket and could see he'd neglected to recharge it fully. If the sky were clear he half-expected he would be able to see his car translated there, as a new constellation. Off in the distance across a vast rhombus of field was a farmhouse with all its lights on and he made his way toward it, across a field that had already been harvested for something and was now in the process of both freezing and thawing. Tractor tires had made thick hard ridges in the dirt, but elsewhere the soil was slippery and he had to watch his step. He knocked on the farmhouse door. A woman answered.

"Yes?" she said. She was wearing a red knit suit jacket with black knit pants. She did not open the door wide but still Finn could see behind her a dozen or so people at desks staring at computer monitors. It was not a home at all but a technology office of some kind. Yet where were the employees' cars? There were none in the driveway. How had they gotten here? Had they tunneled up from underground? And why were they working so late? Perhaps they had all come in the pickup truck that was parked in the barn.

"I've driven off the road and I need to use your phone."

"You don't have a phone?"

"It's dead. Like the car."

"I'll phone the sheriff," she said, starting to close the door.

"My car's right over there," said Finn, pointing into the cold evening air.

"Yes, I see it. Go wait there. The sheriff will be there shortly. And here. Use this Kleenex for your forehead." Her heartlessness reminded him of his own mother, who had been one of those stone-cold nurses the world is full of and probably needs.

He trudged back to the car and sat in it. The litter box seemed strangely to have moved very little, simply slid up against the door. In a few minutes the sheriff's car arrived with its spinning red lights. Festivity or death? Was it Christmas or a car accident? "So what happened here? Spin off the road?"

"Yes, sir."

"A couple other cars have done that tonight." He was writing down a report. "A tow truck is headed this way as we speak."

"Oh, thank god."

"Shouldn't be too long."

"Fifteen minutes?"

"Maybe."

"Do you know what business is in that farmhouse over there?" Finn pointed.

"Nope. Can't say as I do."

"I'd like to recharge my phone."

"Can't help you there. If your car restarts, do you have a recharger in it, one that fits into the lighter space?"

"Yeah, maybe." Finn had already given up on the phone.

"You been drinking?"

"Not at all."

"I believe you," said the sheriff and got back in his cop car. "You take care," he said and sped away.

Finn was just starting to shiver a little sitting in his own car when the tow truck arrived also flashing its red light. This time it was truly like Christmas. Finn jumped out.

"Boy am I glad to see you!" he said, and he went over to hug the man, who was huge and toothless and grimy in overalls. A beautiful man. A man beautiful to behold. Finn wanted to marry him. He never wanted to be without him. He needed a man like this in his life, always and forever.

The man smiled back. "Yep. People are always happy to see me. It's not a bad job. Let's haul this vehicle back on the shoulder and see if it starts up. Will this be cash or credit?'

"Whichever you prefer," said Finn.

The man hitched his long hook and chain to Finn's car and lifted it out.

When Finn got back in with his keys the engine started right up as if it had never died. Several cars drove past.

"I'd let it run for a few minutes before getting back on the road."

"May I kiss you?" The tow truck driver laughed. "Sure," he said. "But only on the cheek."

Finn gave him a peck and the driver laughed again. "Well, it's been quite a night!" said the driver.

Finn handed his Visa to the tow truck driver, who slid it through a reader in his smartphone.

"I'm just a kisser," said Finn.

"Good for you."

"I'm also a hugger." And he went to throw his arms around the driver one more time.

"Jesus effing christ." The driver stood there stiffly while Finn hugged him again and though Finn wanted to lay his head against the driver's shoulder or torso or upper arm, he refrained.

"The world is full of brothers," said Finn, "isn't it. Teeming with them."

"Yep," said the driver, who now looked apprehensive and got in his truck and drove away.

Hours of gray pines against a black sky toward Navy Lake. Outside of town political signs had begun to appear in the fields and then the large country lawns. Once he crossed into town the yards went silent with their opinions. What did that mean for HRC? He arrived many hours after midnight and thus too late for Lily's book group. But, wait, it would gather the next night, he had been told. He exited at his exit, drove through a 24/7 Wendy's, and ate a crispy breaded god-knows-what in a roll that had the spring of memory foam, as he continued in what seemed to be slow motion. The once solid sky had become gauzy, thinning and whitening into something like dawn, as he drove the short causeway across the lagoon part of the lake, the roads empty and the town quiet. Daytime would have to be his night. He entered his half of the rental house noisily and collapsed on the bed and slept in a dark parallel dream-verse of running and hiding among trees. He awoke midafternoon which in autumn in Navy Lake was already close to sunset. He showered, shaved too quickly, fixed some scrambled eggs, then drove slowly to Sigrid's for the group and its news. He was early, so for a short time it would just be Sigrid. He remembered ruefully when Lily had referred to the friends she'd made in the psych ward as "my book group." On the outside, in her life on the outside, she had this actual group, though she often didn't like them much. "They think they are 'sticking it to The Man,'" she said. "They don't know that The Man is not *men*. The Man is them. They think by meeting and drinking wine and pretending to have read the book they are performing quiet ritualized assertions against their husbands."

When she tried to think more kindly about them she said, "They want the world to like them, to think they're both smart and nice—why do they care? I have little interest in that sort of pseudosalvation. I am there for the wine."

Now *he* was meeting with them. Why had she continued with them if she didn't respect them? Lily had said she had never had the girls' locker room gene and thought it deprived her of feminine verbal projects. "Also, when it was my turn to choose the book? My plan was to choose biographies of assassins, so I could keep up with you!" she told him once with glee.

He knocked on the door and rang the bell, both. One obeys one's doom. One can get into a clown suit but one is still simply obeying.

"Thank you for coming," Sigrid said, closing the door behind him. He left his coat on; she hadn't offered to take it.

"I almost missed the house. Didn't you used to have a big tree out front?'

"It got old," she said. "And then there was a storm."

"What has happened?"

"You may want to sit down."

"Oh, my god." He sank down on the couch, his coat still on. The room, the white built-in bookcases, the hardcover books, the Mexican art, the New Mexican art, the one Picasso print whose black lines matched the wrought-iron railing on the staircase in the corner, the furniture in shades called "Dawn" and "Peat" like one's very own friends from elementary school—he had once thought such a jacked-up bespoke-loving home would have cured everything, but he and Lily would only have brought their own difficult and undissected unhappiness into every room. The ladies of the club met here each Tuesday night. He preferred *Frontline* and sometimes so had Lily, who always said she wanted the *Frontline* voice-over guy to speak at her funeral. He now felt here hate and witchiness and emptiness—not his or even theirs—but that of the universe which had somehow gotten in and was swirling around. It shone around the absent ladies in whatever the opposite of a halo was, even though the ladies of the club had not yet arrived. In his head the music of *Frontline* beat its *Mission: Impossible* bass.

"The group is not coming tonight."

"OK."

"Lily has finally done it," Sigrid said.

"Oh, my god," he babbled again. He dropped his face into his hands.

"She had taken a turn again and was not doing well."

He pulled his hands away. He knew Lily like the backs of them—that is, he never looked closely, too busy reading his own palm. But he had loved her always in that necessary, twisted, hurting way. The actual end of her, though he had imagined it, he hadn't imagined thoroughly. "How? How?" His tears became icicles now frozen mid-drip.

"As I said, she was not doing well."

"Why wasn't she in a hospital?"

"She was. Jack took her there. But once she was there she refused to have visitors."

"But how did she get out?"

"She didn't. The doctors wouldn't allow it."

He didn't know why this had been turned into a guessing game. It caused him to stand, his coat still on. "She jumped from the roof," he said.

"No."

He pulled his coat tightly around him. "She seduced the doctor in order to get his belt." He wasn't sure he actually said this aloud. Perhaps he did. For years he had cleared her closets when she accumulated too many belts, their buckles like the stark hissing mouths of snakes.

"So how could she die?" There was a long silence. He sat back down. "How could she have died? They watch you like hawks in there," he said. "They take away everything. Any accessory to death. There aren't even curtains. Not a shoelace or an earring or a hoodie string." Perhaps she hadn't died. She had staged it somehow to escape. He would find her. She would know that. She would know how to do that and this was the signal that she was counting on him to find her.

Sigrid cleared her throat. "The shower."

"They don't allow you to have anything in the shower. Soap on a rope? I don't think so. And there is always a guard at the door."

"She wanted to die."

"Yes."

"The guard can only do so much. They often have their backs turned out of a small sense of privacy."

"What do you mean?"

"Lily wanted very badly to die."

How well he had understood this through the years. Very little on God's earth could entice her into wanting for long to stay on it. Even dressed as a clown as she cheered on others to embrace life with laughter. "Her doctors were useless," Finn said. "They should all have been set on fire in a public square." Statements such as this were why Finn had no friends who were doctors.

Sigrid took a deep breath. "She held her face up to the shower and—filled her sinuses and lungs with water until she drowned."

He did not say anything—muteness seemed to have grabbed his throat until he could choke out only one word.

"Again?" As when the World Trade Center was bombed for the second apocalyptic time, *"Again?"* he had said. She had tried this before and perhaps at this exact hospital. Was this the same place where when he had gone to visit her she had sat shivering in a plastic gown with her doctor's initials written on her brow with a Sharpie? What was wrong with people? Could they never learn? The clown will always repeat and repeat. He sank down onto the sofa.

"She always said the meds made her mouth dry," Sigrid said, clearing her own throat. "But of course that wasn't it." Sigrid came over and sat next to him, but her proximity repelled him, and he shoved himself over to the end of the couch, away from

her, to put his face back into his hands. "Oh, my fucking god."
He began to cry.

"I'm sorry."

"Where is she?"

"They buried her right away at the green cemetery—"

"—ach—"

"—in Verdigris. It was the site she often spoke of."

"No one called me earlier?"

"Jack was there. We didn't know how to handle it."

Finn had been the waning beau for so long he had never
really absorbed being the ex. He was always just waning. But
he could wax! He really could. He had. Every once in a while
the phone would ring and there was Lily's voice and he and she
would wax again. He would take whatever she would offer. He
was not a cold mad moon. He was a circle of light made from
leftover sun.

Sigrid continued. "We probably didn't handle it right. But
with a green burial things move quickly. The unpreserved body
has to be interred right away by law. Plus they had to move
before the ground froze."

Finn stood up but his balance wasn't good. There was fury in
him as well as defeat. A vertiginous combination. Absurdly, he
sat back down. His thoughts were spinning.

"She called me, you know," he said.

Sigrid scooted closer.

He leaned forward on the couch. He picked up a magazine
and put it back down. "Is the rest of the book group coming?"

"No. Not tonight."

"Oh, yeah, that's right." His continued feigned alliance with
Sigrid was purely tactical.

"You and Lily were never on the same page at the same time," she said.

What was she talking about? He then remembered: others did not see his and Lily's as a mutual love and why would they. There were too many jealous bumps, sudden disappearances, pointed rebukes—no one saw theirs as the passion that it was. It looked like weariness and defeat and sometimes it was, but it was weariness and defeat as attachment. It was passion-at-peace, adoration gone awry and away, then returned, love in the armistice, which one never had without a little war. Finn and Lily's love was a shared secret—though *shared secret* was one of those phrases that also meant its opposite. Like *cleave.* Or *overlook.* No one seemed to have seen what he had seen, or known what he had known: that he and Lily were water birds who'd mated for life—and yet often conducted their lives separately in another part of the meadow or the pond. Though in their case the secret lives were not the secret part. The mating for life was the luminous and unguessed-at part. Were he and Lily not one person split in two?—kind of? Their oneness was daily and miraculous but out of view. There was separateness but also the yearning of two halves trying to return. He had merely neglected to propose to her. Why had he not done that? He ought to have done so long ago. He had meant to be with her forever, to guard her from anything that might befall her. But this failure could have been remedied perhaps. Jack! Who was Jack? What one leaves is always a more powerful thing than what one heads toward, which is vague, indistinct. What one leaves is clear and known and solid. Finn was clear and known and solid. What one heads toward is a sliver, a vibration, a glimpse propelled by a question. The destination disintegrates. Could Jack have made her happy?

Perhaps Finn had not even tried, after a while. Happiness was not an idea he and Lily shared. Their love was the idea. When it came to Lily he believed only in beauty and doom and moderate doom-prevention measures.

He disliked Sigrid's overconfident assertions—they could entrap and encircle him if he did not resist. He tried to stay calm. "*Different pages.* These are perhaps the metaphors of the book club?"

"You two had something, I realize that, but it wasn't enough. You were almost never in harmony. She and Jack did a little better but also not enough."

He would not have it that he knew Lily less well than others. Or that he did less well than others such as Jack. He would not accept that Lily had somehow duped him. Because she had not duped him. He had understood her and he would not allow anyone to think that he and Lily were somehow a sham couple cooked up on the afternoon cooking show of his mind. Their love had a deeply private source, somewhat secret even to himself. They had made a long-ago chance meeting—computer repair shop, parking lot, exchange of numbers—into something heat-filled and operatic but which kept retreating backward into searching, the way operas often did.

"She and Jack clearly did *not* do a little better," he said. In arguments Finn had a tendency to trim the terms so finely that he was no longer defending the initial idea but was merely wanting to be right about anything at all, that is, not to be completely wrong. He stood up again. *Besides, what could you possibly know?* he did not say. Instead he said, "Did she leave a note?"

"For you?"

"Did she leave a note for anyone?"

"Doesn't look like it."

The "for you" seemed unnecessarily cruel.

Sigrid stood too and began petting his sleeve. Was she trying to hug him in consolation? Was she flirting with him again?

"I know it's so hard. So hard and unbelievable."

"Don't touch me," Finn said.

But Sigrid kept on.

"I said don't touch me."

Sigrid went over to a table where there was a little plastic hair clip. She pulled her tinselly blonde-flecked hair back, twisted it, and clipped it on top of her head. Soon he knew she would unclip it and it would come tumbling down in a tousled swirl about her strangely preserved face, its skin like cream cheese. Her red lipstick made her mouth a focal point and she used it to listen with, making sound-retrieving grimaces and moues, a fielder with a mitt, a frog nabbing flies, catching every word, storing them in her cheek to eat later. She had always flirted with him, even though anything between them would jeopardize his job, and even anything not between them could as well, if vindictively she turned her spousal power Finn's way, and when last year he'd asked her repeatedly to stop her flirtations she finally wrote Finn an email that said, "Never mind! I prefer my husband. He at least puts his cards on the table." That she'd believed he had any cards at all in this game, let alone a hand he was playing close to his vest, infuriated him. "He's your damn husband—where else is he going to put his cards?" he had written.

"Jack puts his cards on the table, too," she wrote back. Jack was playing the whole blooming field? The entire half-drunk book club? Of course. Jack was just a player. And when this fall

Finn found himself suspended from the school, he wrote Sigrid and her husband both an email asking for an explanation but hers bounced back. She had locked him out for a month and then began to miss him, and unlocked him, but too late: he did not return her messages. Though her emails kept coming. He didn't know how to lock people out. "Awww, Sigrid likes you," Lily used to say with a big fake grin. "It's called unrequited love. Hmmmmm. I'm a little jealous . . ." And he would give Lily the finger and she would give it back.

"You were spared, Finn," Sigrid said now.

"What on earth are you talking about?"

When Lily was alive he could forget about her for a bit and know he'd see her sometime soonish, but now that she was dead she filled up the space of his head like fumes. She was inescapable. But no she was not dead! This all was an enactment of some kind, as it had been once or twice before. This was once more one of her inscrutable whims. Couldn't they see that? He suddenly wondered whether Sigrid was responsible for Lily's death. Buried her too soon. Murdered her with her own hands.

"Spared because—" Sigrid cleared her throat of the phlegm that always seemed to be there whenever she spoke. "They say never look when the body is removed from the house. Or from the building. Never look. Or it will burn into your brain and become the source of never-ending sorrow."

"Who told you that?" asked Finn.

"They say."

He did not ask who they could be. He clutched his own hair in anguish. "Why was she buried so soon?"

"As I said, the green cemetery she had requested in her will requires it." He did not know about her will. "Also there was a deep freeze headed this way and no one would have been able to dig a plot."

"In October?" He had grown dense. All the information was arriving twice.

"The lake has already begun to freeze. I thought I heard the loud quake of it last night. Though I'm sure I'm wrong. But you know how early winter comes here."

"Even George Washington was afraid of being buried alive. He said to wait three days. You only waited one!"

"Ever the history teacher."

"Don't you know that sometimes people are buried too soon and scratch marks are found on the inside of the coffin lid?"

"Are you suggesting Lily might have changed her mind about wanting to be dead?"

"She was always changing her mind about wanting to be dead. Who doesn't? Everyone does."

A long sniffy pause. "There was no lid or coffin. She was buried simply, in a shroud."

"But she wasn't buried with a pair of scissors! No scissors to cut herself free!"

"Good grief."

"Good? You think so? Where is she in that cemetery?"

Sigrid was very quiet for a long moment. "Everything is unmarked except by something natural and compostable. I placed a large grapefruit there. In its entirety. Large and yellow. You may still see that. There is a kind of clearing in the trees . . ."

"Yes. There is always a clearing in the trees."

Finn had sat back down and Sigrid sat next to him again. "Oh Finn."

"Get away from me!" He threw one arm out, accidentally

bumping one of hers. He recalled once more Sigrid's romantic booty-call texts, his replies of "Please don't do this." That was when Sigrid had blocked him and his own requests had come bouncing back to him in mockery. And then the suspension from his job.

Now she glared at him. Her channel had switched. Her mouth was hard and choppy. Half of it was in a weird comma. "I suppose it was hard on you, having Lily go off to fellate another man like that."

Finn pressed his hands together, a cross between applause and a prayer. He stared at her eyes, which had gone fidgety. "Is this a Latin class?" he asked.

She tilted her head. "I'm going to make us some tea. Would you like caffeine or no caffeine? Lemon?"

He did not answer. Sigrid continued, hesitating before getting up and turning toward the kitchen. "Lily is not your own invention," she said. "She is not a character in a play yourself have thought up."

He stood abruptly and left.

The car filled with the smell of an old orange he'd brought from New York, and with the grease from Wendy's, plus the basil and meat odor of the litter box now sliding on the backseat whenever he took a turn. The car seemed to get lost by itself and then find its way by itself. He was hardly driving it—merely gripping it. He would not allow himself to contemplate this new life without Lily: when he gave a thought in that direction, there was no light and nothing growing in it. Had the rupture between him and Lily been completed and now one of them had had to die? Nonsense such as this floated past the front of his brain like a crop duster trailing banner ads. By the time he found the cemetery the horizon was smudged with dusk. Had the clocks been turned back? All the clocks in his life had been turned back. The office of the premises manager had closed at 4:30. But they had not closed the gate at the road, and Finn had been able to drive in as far as the closest parking lot.

How would he find her in this crazy, unmarked field, signaling its dank dim virtue with the absence of metal and stone? He might need a cadre of diviners. He had the New York orange in his hand and put it in his coat pocket. He would wander through the dead grass, looking for a fresh dig, and he would place the orange there in mournful organic honor. He would kick the grapefruit away like a soccer ball. He would make his orange stand guard over the invisible apple tree of her very self. Apples and oranges: if that was what the two of them had always been, well so be it.

He wandered around but saw no grapefruit. He pressed the toe of his boot beneath an intricate shingling of leaves matted to a calico carpet. God only knew how many people had been dispersed beneath his feet. His boot pressed into the dirt to see how hard it was. Some mud stuck to the leather, more dry than wet yet nonetheless a little moist—there was possibility then. Was there evening light enough?

The moon, which had wandered along the path of the absconding sun, had its hiddenness revealed, floating behind the autumn clouds, then in front, as if dodging a searcher with a searchlight. There was some rustling of leaves behind him. He heard a voice say, "I was hoping you'd get here soon."

He felt his heart suddenly pound in his ears. *What rueful ruse is this?* A quote from nothing, but they both sometimes said it anyway.

And so he said it now, like a password. Or, perhaps, a security question, like one's first pet or one's mother's maiden name. Except it came out as simply "What?" Terrible pain flew up in him and spun him.

There was Lily, standing in the dead fleabane, holding a large grapefruit like a globe, her shroud draped around her, a cocooning filthy gown. She seemed to have emerged from a mist that still swirled about her feet. Beneath the shroud she wore some institutional white pajamas. In her familiar stance, but at a list (or had he cocked his own head—she appeared briefly off-balance, waving like a lamprey or a balloon boy at a car dealership), she still had the proud, fabulous guesswork of a tree to match the rose-gold apple hue of her hair. Deliberate. Undone.

Crazed death had not yet made a stranger of her.

She smiled at him with a mouth full of dirt, her face still possessed of her particular radiant turbulence—yet watery, as if he were seeing not so much her face but its reflection in a pond. Her eyes were the dead bone buttons of a white dress shirt. Then suddenly color, their greenish gray, washed into them.

"What kept you?" she asked.

He didn't say, as perhaps he should have, "My brother has been ill."

"They did not stitch your shroud," he said instead. He looked over her shoulder then back over his own to see if someone else were in on this.

"Yes, something of an invitation. Can't ever resist an invitation. I guess I'm like a bad penny," she said. She brushed some bits of leaf from her hands. "Always turning up."

He did not know what to say. He was mute with staring, too stunned to speak.

"A bad penny for your thoughts," she said.

Lividity had purpled the left side of her face. They had buried her in a hurry and on her side. Her coiffure perhaps had lost some tidiness and shine, but he had always loved whatever her hair was, even the clown wigs.

Lily tried again. "Therapy clowns are natural escape artists. But you know that toast we used to make, Here's to mud in your eye? Let's not ever say that again." She put the grapefruit on the ground and wiped her brow with the back of one hand and fussed with the shroud, which had formed a hood at her collarbone. "This is like an infinity scarf gone very wrong," she said then glanced up. Infinity here meant twisted. Plus a wrong turn. They had buried her in her clown shoes. They loomed beneath her mangled white trousers like water skis. Silence descended as if from a bell jar. "I suppose there should be a howling wind."

Finn cleared his throat. "I think there is one." But the air barely moved. Leaves scuttled slowly like crabs across other leaves. "You're in fine fucking fettle for a dead lady." He was waiting for her to start a proper overture in which she would announce all her themes. Resurrection. Despair. Surprise. He knew that possums and birds sometimes faked their own deaths.

Lily shrugged. Or something like a shrug. "I guess death's kind of a spectrum."

"It would appear that way," said Finn.

"Late-stage capitalism." Whatever the fuck that was supposed to mean. Maybe it meant that death really did cost money, that the afterlife like life continued to charge you for things. "Do you know about Schrödinger's cat?"

He knew that it was about the dead and the living lying side by side. Instead he said, "That's not the one where the telling of the thing destroys the thing?"

"No, cats aren't much bothered by that."

"Are you trying to tell me that you're a thought experiment?"

"Oh, Finn, you always knew that." Again, like a tree in wind, her utterances were the thumps of falling apples. "Did you think I had forgotten you?" she asked.

"No." He had no idea what he thought. Everything seemed scrambled and unstable. He studied the hieroglyphs of her eyes which still had something like unworried worry in them, blinking like a warning that was also a party light. Her man Jack had not managed to cast all the vexation out—there was still plenty left for everyone else.

"You actually look well," he lied a little. *I have heard water is very preserving,* he did not say. He spied that winsome whim in her face, and a hint of rueful ruse, as if she were guessing that the *Candid Camera* people would soon appear. In all the years he'd known her, her gaze seldom lost interest in anything. It contained no repudiation of life. Repudiation of life was expressed in almost everything else about her.

"Why thank you. I'm afraid I've let myself go a little." Without showing her teeth, she smiled, continuing to wipe soil from her mouth with the back of her long thin hand. "The worms haven't got me yet. Ugh—there's one." She brushed it off her sleeve. Some larvae clung to her cheek as if to a plum. She seemed simultaneously sinister and comically benign, as if both the past and the present had smashed her within their grip, shattering her only slightly.

Finn kept having to clear his throat. "So—you aren't *deeply* dead." He had suspected it all along—was she not the very soul of ingenuity? Did he not know a conspiracy when he saw one?—and the unbearable, agonizing joy of it burst on like hot lights within him.

"Do I seem it?" Her smile felt the same to him in all its summoned width and wan-ness. "I suppose I'm death-adjacent. So maybe they rushed things. Everyone's in such a fucking hurry to do the right thing. Guess I'm the residual hullabaloo of the well-meaning hinterlands."

"Did you have a change of heart?"

"Changes of heart are my super-power."

Finn exhaled a short snort of a laugh. He tried to keep the bitterness out of it.

She glanced down and kicked at the mist at her feet, perhaps to locate the grapefruit. "Whoa: they buried me in my clown shoes!" Her clown shoes were men's oxfords with floppy glued-on extensions, all painted apple red, the laces like candy canes.

He was filled with the flooding fond missing he could always muster for her. He studied her slightly new bearing. She bore an expression and posture of disequilibrium despite her treeness.

"The shoes are a nice touch," he said. "I think everyone's become a little deranged, but really: a nice touch." The floppy shoes were of course absurd but familiar in that he had seen her in them so many times before. The white worm now twisting on her neck was new, however, as was the silverfish in her hair.

"I'm sorry: covert ops are also my superpower. Plus? They contain the most potential comedy." She pursed her lips. "That was my honors thesis for my therapy clown certification."

"Yes, well, perhaps not all comedy is as therapeutic as a program like that wants to insist on."

"Kids got it."

"Of course kids got it."

She began to study him back. One of her loose, lavender hands hung down at her side while the other clutched her shroud like a shawl. Her body seemed to have settled, like the contents of a suitcase are said to shift during flight. There was flattening and twisting, new angles and a slight stoop. "You have remained very handsome, I have to say."

"Losing my hair," said Finn, anxiously palming his head.

"You always thought that. Only a little true. Besides: it looks distinguished."

"I cut it."

"Yes, well. You know you're not supposed to cut your hair while your beloved is at sea."

He could also point out to her that he had shaved rather quickly. He rubbed his chin with his hand. "It's been almost a year," Finn said. After a decade of living together he had not seen her since last New Year's Day. "I didn't know where my beloved was. I didn't know what sea."

"Should I not have pursued my existence?"

"I was pretty much abandoned, Lily, like the lamb tail that gets tourniqueted and left to dry and drop off the lamb."

"I was the lamb tail."

"No, Lily. You were the lamb." There was sternness in his voice. "You were the lamb on the go."

"Yes, well, maybe, the black sheep. I guess I'm now just death's useful idiot. Death gets bored and sometimes wants to travel. Wow, look at me." She pressed one hand against her abdomen. "They might have found my organ donor card. I might not have a liver." She moved the white shroud and revealed a bloody bandage.

"Are you serious?"

"I guess I better not drink."

At dinner parties long ago she had often gotten talking to

the people on either side of her and begun to drink their wine. Soon three wineglasses would be arranged around her place setting, all with her lipstick smudges on their rims.

"I'll drink for both of us," Finn said. "Not a problem."

She continued brushing dirt from her sleeves. "Forgive me: a change of clothes before seeing you might have been smart. Sorry. Do I have mushrooms growing out of my eyes or anything?"

"Your eyes are clear."

"Good. That's what it feels like to me." She plucked some strands of hair off her brow with two twiggy fingers.

He cleared his throat and shifted his weight. "Are you still on Facebook?"

She was quiet for a moment. "That's what you have to say to me?"

"No, I have other things."

"But aren't you happy to see me, Finn? I did go to some effort. I did."

Though her teeth and lips had the blue-black tinge of a merlot drinker, as if she'd been celebrating underground, her face held the same prettiness it always had. It was a face whose occasional ordinariness could slide momentarily into homeliness, or another time, with her hair piled up and the sun shining, appear impossibly beautiful and light. You had to stick around for the show. The large apple tree aspect seemed combined now with her horse look: her horse's bangs stick-straight and disarrayed, dipping into her large, seeing eyes which had no blind spots except a horse's two, directly ahead and directly behind: this is where, unfortunately, Finn had always stood with her. He could never manage the sides.

"You didn't leave a note."

"Finn. Suicide notes! Everyone knows they're full of shit."

"So. OK. I'm still trying to work this out. Did you hold your breath and just play dead?" Perhaps death was like a wrestling match: the referee could be on his hands and knees watching the pin closely but slap the mat too soon. He knew with near drownings sometimes the heartbeat and pulse remained too faint for detection. He forced a quick grin which probably looked frightened or mean though he hoped not.

"Are you going to make me do a TED Talk about my devious inner world?" She paused. "I mean, I guess I just don't have the gene for prolonged slumber." She repeated very faintly, "Finn, aren't you happy to *see* me?"

"Happy?" Was he supposed to celebrate with his whirling dance routine with which he'd once in their long-ago youth regaled her? All verbal strength, all fabrications, fell from him. He was consumed by a feeling of nakedness, his through-the-years uneasing ache for her, a sense of leaving his body altogether, his heart flying out the back of his own neck. This came and went and he was soon mostly back in his body again to resume the role of village moron. And then not. The empty asphalt parking lot that sometimes set up shop in his chest, like a thing bombed in wartime then paved over, flew off and away. Snow fell in silence. "Oh, my god. Lily." He stepped toward her tentatively. He hoped he did not seem furtive or ambivalent as he approached her. "Right this second? I am the happiest man on the planet." He was eager to touch her, but he did not want to scare her or himself. He froze and resumed a posture of indifference, as best as he could recall one. "I'm also happy at the money I'm going to save not having to have your death portrait painted from my screen saver."

"Ha!" she said.

Actually, he had changed his screen saver from a photo of Lily to a photo of Hillary Clinton, but he wouldn't tell her that. Nor would he tell her about all the little gift items he had seen in shops and bought for her, things he knew she would love but would never buy herself or ever again encounter, things that he wanted to please and surprise her with then realized he could not—and so he always saved the receipts and returned them. So he had saved some money there as well.

Nor would he tell her how furious he was at her for her death nor how through the years prior there had been moments he had wished she would just get it over with and go ahead and not mull so dramatically and create all that dread in him. He would not tell her how she had worn him down any number of times until he had thought, Well just die then, if that's what you need. He would not report to her now that she and her illness, which had lived in her like an exotic poisonous pet, had reduced him to heartlessness. And though he bounced back, he would often find it all hard to forgive—forgive the thing she became and the thing she had turned him into.

But now he just stepped toward her.

"No," she said, stepping back.

"I can't hold you?" His heart, a fucked-up creature in a cage, flung itself against his ribs.

"No!" she said. "I'm not sure! I, I don't think so . . . no."

The late fall smell of applewood burning. Was this her very flesh? Flakes of snow continued to fall silently from the sky like the third act of *La Bohème*. It gathered on his shoulders in epaulets. He wanted to throw himself on the ground and stick a knife in his eye. Frozen, standing there, he felt a heaving within himself—the weeping inside came out. He felt his mouth stretching in a wide line and he began to sob. And then so did she, at her chosen distance, their cries suspended then drifting in the air between them. He stepped toward her in a slow automatic way.

"No!" she said again. She tried to switch gears. "Did you know that *flange* means 'undesirable vagina'?"

"I've missed you."

"Thank you. Perhaps true love has trouble in life but navigates death rather well."

He stepped toward her again, and this time she did not move back and soon she was slumped against him and he held her, with some deep and unnameable emotion, stepping on the immense shoes, his hands in her hair, his coat sleeves around her thin, muddy, cold apparel made familiar with her old perfume. Iris and frankincense against the new leathery scent of her skin. Perhaps her old scent had preserved her. Someone must have sprayed it on her. His arms felt the muscle memory of her in them, or perhaps it was the memory of muscle memory. Her thin hands with their branching blue veins roamed all around his body. Her touch was a balm. Crazed dying had not yet made a stranger of her. Their lips meshing, their teeth smashing, their tongues lost in greeting: the sound of their weeping began to louden with confusion and betrayal.

"What happened?"

The air now filled with strangled agonized phrases which at first stuck in their throats and then escaped, circled, floated. "What do you mean what happened?" During pauses the words seemed muffled and done but were not.

Fuck Sigrid and the book group: he and Lily had always been on the same page. They were part of a quantum entanglement. They were spooky actions at a distance, a genuine unified theory of the universe. This was all he knew of physics and perhaps of love.

"What did you do?" he asked. "You took your one mortal life and tossed it away."

"Apparently not."

"But perhaps." He pulled a stinkbug from her sleeve. "I looked everywhere for a sign of you. I've seen your face in clouds and oil slicks and puddles and downpours of rain . . ."

She closed her eyes. "Oh, Finn, let's not get poetic."

"What did you do?"

"I'm not sure," she said, her face now stretched with anguish against his coat, her mouth mashed against his sleeve. She pulled herself away, at arm's length, as if she were trying on a new bright tone of voice. "You know, children's theater is mostly participation plays: you leave holes in the play to allow the audience to contribute." She grew quiet. "Didn't you try to forget me?" she asked.

He was startled and stepped back from her, but still holding her at that same arm's length she had attempted. "You didn't give me enough time!" he cried. He looked around as if he'd forgotten where he'd put something. He looked back at her beautiful but not especially well face. "Your sepulchral silences in the play. I guess I just couldn't read the room."

"I am so sorry," she said. "You can leave now and say you never saw me."

"At this point I think that would be impossible."

"Nothing is impossible."

"What *is* this ghastly place?"

"The green cemetery," she said. "It's a little Keep America Beautiful, I suppose. Very environmental. If you . . . like the environment. And would like to be one with it."

"Cremation's not green?"

"Cremation's very extreme." He was forcing her to participate.

"Might deter suitors?"

She stared at him.

"Too much downsizing?"

"An urn, yes, is playing very hard to get. Also cremation has beaucoup carbon emissions. And the ash scattering? Litter."

"I thought you wanted the body farm? The one near Alabama or wherever? Both of us, with our banjos on our knees? I thought we were both going to do that because our fathers had once worked in law enforcement and we were going to contribute to forensic science, et cetera, et cetera, et cetera?"

"What is wrong with you?" she said moving toward him again, gently gathering his face in her hands.

Again, he pulled away from her. "What is wrong with *me*?" This would no longer be a moonlit clearing. This would no longer be a magic little meadow. "Number one: this *place*? Has a visitors' center. It has a visitors' center that is closed and so they can't hand out maps to unmarked graves. Maps to unmarked graves! *That* is what is wrong with me, Lily!"

She glanced at the low-hanging branches. "Yes. I suppose it could use a string of chili pepper lights."

"Number two: you are covered in dirt—you're caked with it."

"I guess I made my spot on god's cold earth a little uncomfortable and now it's returning the favor." She brushed again at her shroud. "Perhaps not such a great awakening after all. Not the fresh m.o. I was going for. Just another creature of the necroscape. Not shiny with resilience and invention as I'd hoped."

"There are clots of snow and shit in your hair which, by the way, is like a big unraveled mitten of yarn. Your vitals are not so vital, but yes! Yes! What is *wrong with me*?"

"You didn't keep an eye on me."

"I didn't keep an eye on you? That is the most ludicrous—"

"—no, you didn't—"

"—thing I've ever heard!"

"—not really, you didn't really."

Was she right? He had thought about her constantly but perhaps had not gone looking. "I did nothing but want you," he said fiercely.

"It's not the same."

But it would have to suffice, for then and for now, since there had been nothing else sane for him to do. Now insanity had come to him and caught them both in this strange late dusk dream, which was like a daydream but with more solidity, less light, and more doubt. "It's getting cold," he said. She was shivering. The soundless snowflakes continued to float down. How often he had loved the cold, the winter mornings with Lily in bed, under quilts, the bright sun in the blue sky, brilliantly reflecting off the snow, long thick icicles glitteringly cross-hatched with the venetian blinds. Winter had been his favorite time with her, and if ever he would leave her, he hoped it would not be in any actual season.

She pulled away, still shivering. "Look. I'm sorry this isn't a lovely sunlit garden with psalms being recited by children who have flowers in their hair and fat songbirds all about. I'm sorry there is just this fucking devouring mud . . . in deep twilit October . . ." She pointed to a spot about twenty feet away. The ground cover was a prickly invasive losing its green. "You see that grave over there? Well, you don't because it's not allowed to be marked. But every day people bring food to it and just place it there. And when they go away, a homeless person comes in to eat it. Sort of like cookies for Santa Claus."

"I won't ask you how you know all that."

"I have heard the food bringers speaking," she declaimed.

He wondered why they hadn't taken the grapefruit.

He stepped toward her. It was just too cold not to. He could smell the one tooth in her that collected her morning coffee and smelled now and again of swamp sulfur. In some manner or other she was always having her head devoured by darkness and decay.

The snow was collecting in her hair and eyelashes, sticking like confetti. Ah, here was their wedding! Then, as if his thought had been heard, a sudden wind came sweeping in, with its oceanic sound and its quick picking up of things and taking them elsewhere in a purposeful hurry that was also a bit random.

"Let's get out of here," he said, and grabbed her cold and bony hand, which had always been cold and bony and he had always liked that, though he had never warmed a ring and slid it on her. Why not? She had never asked. And so he had never had to scrounge around for a reply.

If she had donated her body to medical science, her hands with their now oyster-gray nails would already have been chopped off. Perhaps he would have been given a pair of her gloves, as a memento, and he would have worn them around, his hands inside of them, soft, as if inside of her. And he would have gone through life like that for many very sad years.

"Where are we going?"

To the body farm in Knoxville. A crickety town with sad spaghetti. They would drive tentatively in that direction, which had been her wish as he understood it.

"Someplace where it doesn't snow in October. Thank god the science is still out on climate change or this freakish winter might be worrisome. We might think it's the polar ice caps melting and sending us their cooling air before everything goes up in flames."

"I might melt though, going south." She walked hesitantly, leaning against him. "Still, it's true: I'm freezing cold."

"Are you hungry?" he asked, and she just gave him a look that was part *Are you kidding? Of course not* and part *Are you kidding? Of course.* He picked up the grapefruit.

She could move reasonably well. He helped her into the passenger seat of his car, placed an old blanket he had in the back over the entirety of her body, leaving her face to peek out, and then started up the engine, without the headlights, so that they were floating in the night, out of the green cemetery with fewer carbon emissions. He tried not to think that what he was doing could be misconstrued as body-snatching. She pulled down the visor to catch a glimpse of herself in the lighted mirror.

"This mirror is gaslighting me," she said.

He pressed his foot on the accelerator and the car lurched forward against the natural spin of the earth and then seemed to cause the earth to reverse rotation and carry them forward. Lily's head did a small smack against the seatback.

"Y'okay?"

"Fine as dust," she said. "Ha-ha." All her laughs contained actual "ha-has" but not all her "ha-has" contained actual laughter. This one was an admixture in the second "ha."

He had studied her too much and too aimlessly through the years, and perhaps it had wrecked his mind.

The car rocked along the rutted dirt drive. Gravel smashed occasionally under the tires and a stone or two flew up and hit the underbody of the car. Its suspension seemed in doubt for a second. She closed her eyes the way she always had when the ride got bumpy. He noticed there was blue and purple around the sockets and also around her ankles above the clown shoes. Even in death the body had hope and sent blood. "Are we there yet?" she asked. "The research farm?" They were not even out of the Verdigris driveway. Her eyes stayed closed. Perhaps this was how she looked when dead, which, when you got right down to it, he had still not really seen. Her face had the appearance of a deceitful peace.

Once they hit the highway he turned on the headlights and cranked up the car heat. She said nothing through all of this, and the heater kicked in and fluttered the part of her shroud that stuck out from beneath the blanket. Her big red shoes barely fit into the footwell in front of her, but she did not take them off. "You're right: the shoes were certainly a nice touch. Though I'm sure they didn't play the theme from *Mission: Impossible,* as I had requested. They probably just played some damn Bach."

"It was outside. So I was told. In some early snow. Earlier than this. I don't think there was much music."

"They didn't play 'When I Marry Mister Snow'?"

He positioned his mouth in a tight smile. "Don't think so."

"I also wanted 'I Won't Dance Don't Ask Me.'"

"I know you did."

"'Sing, Sing, Sing' would have been good. Benny Goodman is always rousing. Also, 'Will You Still Love Me Tomorrow.' Every dead person wants to know."

Finn cleared his throat a little. "I guess when you drown yourself you can lose some say in the details of what happens next." He said this neither slowly nor with feeling.

"Are we there yet?" she asked again.

"Tomorrow," he said. "We'll be there tomorrow."

"Hmmmmm. Have you ever noticed how weird the word *tomorrow* is?"

"As a concept?"

"No, as a concept it's fantastic. I mean the look of it as a word on the page. It's like a word from some strange made-up language. Part Italian. Part Apache. Do you still have satellite radio?"

"First you're dead and now you want satellite radio?"

"Sorry."

Did she just apologize? Maybe he was hallucinating. He so badly wanted her to say she was sorry. About anything. Anything at all. Not just the mud. Not just the radio.

"I didn't renew my subscription. In time," he added.

"Is this a zombie movie?" she asked a little sadly.

"Nah. Subscriptions are always renewed in those."

"Is it a rom-com?"

"Maybe."

"Perhaps it's a documentary. A sweet documentary. With a bit of thriller in it."

Ahead he would take a right at the uncoiling ribbon of county road. They would then be on the lam. "A western with a heist—a prison break."

"They went thataway!" said Lily with a daft grin.

"Hang on to your hats," he replied, gunning the engine. He felt a kind of small joy he had never felt before—an amalgam of old joy and new. Although that was the thing with joy: it was constantly presenting itself as an unprecedented feeling. Every time, you had never felt like this before.

"If anyone is on the lookout for us we will be like Heisenberg's electrons—we'll have speed but no discernible location," he said. "The moral of every story, boys and girls, is that you never really know where anybody is."

"A science special. I love those," she said.

And though the science perhaps was still out on love, he felt that every couple was absurd and brought out the absurdity in each other. Were they themselves not the quasi-living proof?

Heat from the car blasted onto their legs. Lily began to tell a short tale. "I once saw a lady gorilla trying to get the attention of a robot gorilla. She used a saw just like the indefatigable robot did, copying him, but then she grew very tired when he didn't stop sawing and pay some attention to her. In fact he didn't in her presence change one thing about himself at all. He was a robot. But he was a male robot. And so, though she tried her best, she grew tired and a little bored and laid her head down on the saw for a while. Then she picked her head up and loped away."

"What are we really talking about here?"

"Nature," she said. "Perhaps. Is this a dream? Where am I? Where are you?"

"Right now? We're deep in the theme from *Valley of the Dolls.*"

There were state lines ahead to cross and they would cross them. Lily pretending to be dead! Surprise! Ha! Ha! Was this not evidence that living was funny?

In the coppery dark they passed a lake that was beginning to freeze but was not yet frozen. A hundred migrating swans had found plenty of water in it for landing. The sound and sight of them caused him to ease up on the gas. "Look!" he said, slowing, then stopping on the shoulder of the road. Snowflakes still fell but instantly disappeared on landing.

"Oh, the migrating swans! It's their time. It's that time of year." The swans would migrate, lake to lake, going south, their mezzo honks jaunty and low like a thousand geese playing a thousand muted tubas. Some of the swans seemed insistent on a bass note from a different key, nicely fritzing out the chord.

"I don't think I've ever seen that many swans before," said Finn. "Not so many!"

"Really?"

"Yeah. I hope it's not global warming."

"Who knows," she said. "A lot of strangely beautiful things are. Lots of thawing and rising and psychedelic sunsets."

What was she implying? That she too, her own defrosting, was climate change at work?

They stayed for a minute more, listening to the swans complain, sing, put their unresolved harmonics unfeasibly into the air. Then he and Lily moved on into the night, the car humming, the road unspooling once more before them.

At one point, perhaps it was just after they passed a sign that read LOW SOFT SHOULDERS, Lily pressed close to Finn as he was driving. "You're a good-looking man," she said. "Y'always were."

She laid her head in his lap and then, with her mouth swelled open and inverted like a sea creature, she turned and began to move, knead, nurse against him, undo his zipper, and kiss some more. All this was familiar in the most heart-pounding way. They were both themselves and not themselves, chimerical and confused. Their sexual life seemed from a long ago and far dark lagoon. "Oh, Lil, I don't know . . . ," he said, but he did not stop her. The tendons strained beneath her neck. He was an organism taking the shape of whatever moved through him. "I think this is a crime in several states." He found a rest stop—or was it a runaway truck ramp—and just pulled the car over. He turned off the ignition. He found the lever that flipped the back of his seat flat in the car.

Just as she used to early in their relationship, she gently took off his clothes: "This is so happening," she had said then and said again now. "You can resist but only a little." She was not to be resisted. Her kisses had teeth in them. "Too much consent is a buzzkill," she whispered. "But a little is good. I just hope I'm not a horror to you." Now she would give him the home remedy of love. Her shifting organs and her stoop would be of use in this particular situation. He would avert his gaze from the lavender piping of veins in her brow. The heat from the car was mean and fine. She was a spirit now. They were again enmeshed and entangled.

"I haven't had a surprise like this since the Clinton administration," he was interested to hear himself say.

"I put some perfume in my hair—a few days ago," she said and then became an ecstatic bag of bones. Her lips had the shimmer and slip of fish skin. He was careful how he held her.

"I'm running over with lovely thoughts," he said. He was happy for their love. He was happy for happiness. He was cuckoo for Cocoa Puffs—an expression people didn't use anymore but probably should.

He had been beguiled briefly from mourning. Her mouth became a splodge of jam. All this desire suffused with love was not desire any longer since possession made it entirely love.

He noticed another silverfish in her perfumed hair. And then he shut his eyes completely and went offline for a bit. When he came to, he no longer knew anything.

"Lily, you are ruthless," he found himself murmuring with affection and gratitude—he was without power, so he wasn't sure, but for a moment it felt like unquellable happiness.

"I am so sorry," she said, "that in our years together I was unable to wake every day with a song in my heart." She smelled like warm food cooling. Sorrow had entered her face and her mouth split into the downturned clownish crescent it used to take her professional makeup to produce. "At least not the right song."

"It's OK," he said, bringing her into his arms.

The most evolved invertebrates, the most equivalently evolved biological Others, such as octopus or squid, also had divided their species into males and females. Was it such a terrible, overly creative, excessively hopeful idea? On the other hand, the most advanced Others such as squid also had three hearts and a brain wrapped around their throats. Who couldn't use three hearts and a neckerchief brain? Finn could use all of it.

He and Lily had lost each other long ago, and now they woke up every hour or so to look in anguish out the windows and flood the car interior with their grief.

Darling sister,

Here I sit by the lantern with its chicory blue flame. It shines off the oak desk that I just this morning polished with cold tea. I have recently taken to having a little claret in the evenings with the gentleman boarder Jack. He sometimes adds a pinch of powder to his and offers me the same. I have said yes to the powder now twice and pretend I don't know it is opium of a fine grade—he is a touch proud—stronger than the usual housewife powder and good for sleep, baths, reading the scripture, and staring at the additional ambrotypes I found in a crate on the porch of an abandoned house years ago and which I have been using to mend the broken windowpanes in some of the rooms upstairs, as I may have mentioned. Moonlight sets them quite to life. And the late afternoon sun, when it is horizontal and diffuse, even more.

Mr. Jack once told me he felt he had a lot to offer as a man. He meant in a woman's eyes. That he had a lot to offer a woman. But when men say this and they don't mean a fine house in a fine town I just think, Hmmm-hmmm.

Still I pray for features such as goodness and gentlemanly

indulgence. I have had to refreshen day old biscuits with steam and hot skillet grease. In all ways, if you know what I mean.

As I said to the pastor once, "I believe it's not the prayer, it's the things you do to help the prayer along that gives the prayer a fighting chance."

He said, "No man of faith would know what to say to that."

And I said, "Well, then no man of faith would argue. Faith is not about argument."

"Well, Miss Libby, men of faith love to argue, I'm afraid."

"Well, that's a bit of a contradiction of character, don't you think?" Since that is how it seems to me.

"Oh, I'm not so sure," he said with an indulgent smile.

"I believe the scriptures are like crossword puzzles. The clues aren't really clues just confirmation when you figure it out some other way."

"That is certainly one way of looking at it," he said.

"But I gather not the correct one."

Earlier in the day the handsome boarder hiked downstreet past the wheelwright's to the printer's shop to get a copy of the newspaper from St. Louis, the newspaper from Memphis, and the newspaper from Chicago. "Have to find out if I've been arrested or if I died or got married or perhaps for some reason have been elected governor." He wore a silk ascot for this errand and kept it on all day.

"Well, here you be," I said when he returned. "Guess life's been uneventful." A shadow crossed his face. "Or your publicity mistaken."

"Maybe so," he agreed and left the newspapers in the receiving parlor for the other lodgers.

But it has aggrieved me the way he is around Ofelia. Unseasonably cold then unseasonably warm. Both of them have come to me with their weather reports.

He says, "Does she stay overnight here?"

I tell him I sometimes allow it, if it's more convenient for her. "There's no cause for unkindness."

"She's under the same roof. God has made distinctions among us!"

These are the moments I begin slowly then quickly to despise him.

"God has gone horseback riding," I say, "and we are left behind to tend to one another."

"Well, aren't you the heathen." He smiled.

"I don't care much for horseback riding."

"Too much hucklebuck?"

That sort of remark is when I try to find something else I must do. Pies to make and curtains to mend.

"I think you should join me in a recitation some night," he said with some slyness.

"Mercy!"

"You dipping your toe into show business would put light and joy into the hearts of simple benighted men."

"I believe you've said something like that before. And I wasn't having it then."

"Well, I should get myself a real actress."

"Indeed you should."

And we left it there.

I think of you often, missing you so, and wondering what you would do given this or that or this and that yet again.

Yours every time,
Eliz.

He fetched a shirt and corduroy pants from the suitcase he'd left in his car and helped her put them on. "Where do you think we should head for now? The way we were already going?" The roads were clear sailing. Everything had to start somewhere. Except eternity, which shot out in all directions endlessly and so had no such spot. "I may need stops and snacks," she said. "Perhaps we should go snackward."

"There will be some on this route to the body farm."

"Where everyone goes when they're running away." She paused. "Kind of southwest: land of the runaways. I'm cool with that. Not that I have a compass or a choice."

"People don't have compasses anymore."

"Some do," she said, clearly just to argue.

"We'll do celestial navigation. We go more east than west. The clayey moon and the sugary stars. I'll look for the Southern Cross." As if he knew anything about the Southern Cross. He had a faint recollection it wasn't even in the Northern Hemisphere. "If you start to feel kidnapped let me know."

She sighed. "I always feel kidnapped. Hit the road, Jack. I mean—you know what I mean."

"Maybe," he said.

She rolled down her window and cool air freshened the car. She called out of it, to the passing countryside, "Apologies to all you actually kidnapped people out there! But a couple of you will know what I mean!" Then she rolled the window back up.

"Ever the therapist."

"Ehn."

"I'm going to do a mix of small roads for scenery and cop avoidance and interstates for speed."

"You are fantastic."

"At this point, we're both a little fantastic."

There was a tiny smile on her lavender lips. "I suppose."

The trees sped by them on either side. The mad, bald head of the moon rose over the purple mountains' majesty, no arguing with that. They must have been in Kentucky by then, though he didn't recall having crossed the milky herbal tea of the wide Ohio so who knew. Night deepened and fell. In the sky, however, there was that moon river again, wider than a mile, its name excised and replaced with Lily's. He usually did get all the moon songs mixed up.

"It's only a paper moon," said Lily, in her papery attire, which she had laid over the shirt and corduroys like a dental patient.

He fiddled with the radio dial but didn't get much. As they drove, Finn would glance quickly and get to see Lily, bestirring herself in and out of sleep, over and over. This repetition of her reelectrified life exhilarated him, her beauty thrilling in its contradictory yet familiar ways——confusion in the brows, calm along the mouth, her seeking him with one eye only, the other at rest behind its veiny lid. Her hands gnarled and violet but with golden vellum in the webbing between her thumbs and forefingers.

She sniffed under her own arms. "Hmmm. The terroir on Verdigris Road is not so great," she said. "I guess I forgot to tell everybody I really wanted to be buried at the forensic farm. I guess I forgot to tell anybody."

"You told me. But it seemed very hypothetical at the time."

"I suppose it was. But burial is always hypothetical until suddenly it's not. I want my death to be helpful. Even if it turns out it's not. I want to try to be helpful. Has that not been my basic principle in life? My basic principle which I always mangle?"

"It did get mangled," he said. And then he changed the subject though not really. "Did you put your things in order?"

"What things?" She was peeling the grapefruit.

"Your affairs," he said, quietly, pointedly. "Did you put your affairs in order." Did he mean Jack? He wasn't sure.

"What are you doing, Finn," she murmured. She put a grapefruit segment in her mouth and then one in his.

"I don't know," he mumbled, feeling the citrus burst sweet and sour. It seemed to have no seeds. Barren fruit. In nature, he once read, only the tapeworm and the albatross were monogamous. Everything else was interested in a lot of seeds.

Lily looked around her seat, the grapefruit peels scattered on the floor mat. "I don't have a purse. That is sort of a bummer. I hope you don't mind paying for things. Also? Do you have a comb? I really need a hairbrush but that may be too much to ask for."

He maneuvered a comb out of his back pocket while driving with one hand. Was that not circus-level talent? "Here," he said.

"Thank you. All those years of life and I never got the hang of my hair."

"I doubt death has cleared it up for you."

She was quiet. As if they were not supposed to speak of her having died.

She began combing her knotted and yam-hued hair. To get her back into shape they would need a dry, well-heated room, some grooming utensils, and a commitment to Pilates, to prevent the whole compost thing from overtaking her. She once more pulled the car visor down to look at herself in the mirror. She pinched her own cheek. "Could use a little plumping with ballistic gelatin. My dad's line of work."

"I know," he said. Her father had been in forensics. His father had had a desk job. But both cops. Her father had been mildly schizophrenic. Good cop. Bad cop. She used to like to make that joke.

"I mean, Lily," he said driving in the night. "Did you really die?"

"Perhaps I got stuck in the revolving bardo door," she said. "Not sure. I think the whole thing might be a slippery slope where if you get enough traction you can get back up the slope."

The cat box shifted around in the back of the car.

She turned to look. "You've been living in your car?" she asked.

For someone who'd been living in the dirt, it seemed highhanded and insensitive.

"No, what makes you think that?"

"No one has a cat box in their car unless they're living in their car. With their cat."

"I don't have a cat."

"Whoa. Man, Finn, that's even worse. That's like— Well, I can't even think about it."

He would give her a smile, if she looked his way, but as he

kept the peripheral vision of his right eye on her he could see that she was just looking straight ahead.

He turned on the radio so they could listen to possible reports on melting glaciers and rising sea levels and award nominations for best performance in a comedy or a musical.

"You didn't get another cat when Crater died?" she finally asked. They had named their cat after the famous judge. In honor. In honor of reappearances.

"Regrettably, no," he said. For the rest of his life he could begin every sentence with *Regrettably* and never tell a lie.

"I suppose a dog would be better?"

"Probably. You look to a dog to see how to be happy. You look to them to learn how they know that the world's a good place."

"You look to cats to watch them come and go and come and go."

He kept driving into the night, following his own headlights. Was there anything else a person could do? "Do you believe the stars can steer our lives?" he asked.

"Of course," she said. "Who wouldn't believe that?"

"The stars just seem like a mess to me." He sighed. "A hundred million billion stars—and still not infinite."

"I guess it will have to do. It will have to suffice as infinitude."

"Guess so."

"They shine. They sparkle. They share space. They have manners. Do you think each of these gazillion stars could be a person who died?"

"Each of these stars is a star that died. Or could be. Are they in conversation? Part of a design? They each seem unaware of the others. And since you don't know whether they're dead or alive—their lives are many years further back than their look of life—their shine for us on earth is all the same whether we're looking at dead shine or live shine. Starlight is simply performative."

"You always lacked a little romance."

"Not at all," he insisted. "It's just when I look at the stars I notice the frightening space between them: that space is what we travel through in life. That inner space? It's also outer space. And though it's called 'outer space,' it takes place on earth. The stars themselves are a tease and a taunt."

"This was why we were in couples therapy."

"Let's not talk about that." He felt the static electricity, the clash of preshattered wills.

"OK. Let's go where there are some sycamore trees," she said. "Encompassing, enmeshed sycamores."

"All right. Let's do that."

"The world is being reintroduced to me."

"And reissued. And reanimated. For me."

"I'm sorry to be taking you away from your brother," she said.

Had they spoken about this? He couldn't recall. It was the vampirism of the beloved. It was her ventriloquized and mumbling heart. It was the space between the stars. It was also like the stars themselves which sat there invisible in the day. It took the disappearance of sunlight to see what had been there all along. Like the matter of his brother.

"Don't worry about my brother," said Finn. "I've got him covered. I may not be there. But he's here in my heart. And I'm getting back to see him soon."

"You will blame me for distracting you."

"No." A small night animal darted across the road. Not enough of a waddle for a raccoon, thus indecipherable.

"What was that?" she asked, then yawned, the slight rot smell of her mouth escaping into the car. As her mouth fell closed again he noted in passing that the darknesses between her teeth were not decay but little spaces revealing the never-ending cavity of her throat.

"Just don't let weariness set in. You're supposed to keep me awake while driving. Navigator's task." But weariness had already settled in and she was slumping against him and not in a good way.

"Navigator. Hmmmm." She closed her eyes and sighed. "I wish we had a guidebook. And don't say, 'There's no guidebook for this.' I could hear you about to say that." Now she was mumbling and her slump became accentuated.

"Did you know that deep in the Mariana Trench—"

"Didn't you date her in high school?" Lily murmured, wagging one clown shoe. "Darien Gap's cousin? Ha-ha. Will this do for navigation?"

"—scientists found fossils possessed of DNA that had begun to grow the dead fossilized creature back, that a circulatory system had begun to appear? And the entire organism was presumed to be in the process of coming back to life."

"Really?" Lily straightened and spun her pale head toward him, pearl-clutching his near arm with her far one.

"Well, that woke you up," he said. The knobs of her right wrist had shot out the sleeve of the shirt he had put on her, and her long fingers clung to his arm until they loosened again, and she sank back, seemingly asleep. Gray spittle collected in the corners of her mouth.

Finn felt a nauseous hunger in him which the grapefruit had not assuaged. "We could use some crackers," he said now. "And don't say we're going to see those living alongside this road."

But suddenly, like a bird who could bring about half-hemispheric sleep, Lily was in a snore that seemed to emanate from deep inside. Her jaw was twisted to reveal her teeth, her mouth continued its widening like meat on a spit, her limbs in a swastika like a marionette's. Which parts of the spasming body really belonged with the body? Cubism was right! The shroud had slid, and his shirt on her was now hiked up and her ribs resembled the slats of venetian blinds behind the translucent voile of her skin. How could this be the woman he loved? And yet it was.

"Ritz, maybe," said Finn to keep himself driving. "The salt and malt. That's what gives them their *je ne sais quoi*." He cleared his throat. "As they say at the Ritz itself. Where the crackers were invented. Maybe." He had been teaching too long. He was able to talk to himself for long stretches. He made up too much and hoped for the best, like every teacher.

They would soon perhaps have to be looking for a Homewood Suites. That was more likely where Ritz crackers were invented. He was wondering whether she was awake.

"Are you done?" she murmured from her now one-eyed doze.

"Probably not," he said. He let many minutes go by. "I think we're lost," he said, though of course she had gone back to sleep.

He let her sleep, and when she stirred and woke yet again she seemed suddenly electrified with mechanical moves, like a Fosse dancer.

"I think I broke my ankle in the shower," she said.

"Broke your ankle? That's what you think you did?"

"It was a little slippery."

"Mmmmmm. Perhaps we should get it looked at."

"Are you joking?" she asked. "Sometimes I can tell but not always."

Finn let a long silence sit between them.

"So what *is* death like anyway?" he asked finally.

"Kind of what you think. And kind of not what you think." She leaned toward him with her big stinking smile. "It's sort of what you make of it."

Her eyes glittered with the iridescent green of a peacock tail or a fly. Her face often caught the light that way at night. She continued. "But through it all, my love never died. Not everything when you die dies all at once and together. And some things flicker back on. You kind of get trapped in this partial power outage. The guys with helmets fix some things but not others." She sighed. "You think you can be the artist of your own death but surprise! You can't even be the artist of your own art. It always turns out crappier than you planned."

Loss of the heart kills the brain, he had read. Loss of the brain kills the heart. But only eventually. A million love stories demonstrated it! The heart could go on and on. Love was its own little generator of quasi-buried treasure.

"Did you bring any weed?" asked Lily. "It hurts a little, the deadness coming back to life."

"You're the second person this week who has asked me if I have weed."

"So you don't."

"I'm a high school teacher. Or used to be."

"Does that mean you did bring some or didn't?"

"Nada."

"Hmmmmm. Maybe when we next stop somewhere for gas you can get me a cigar. I would like a cigar sticking between my teeth as I talk."

This was the nutty part of Lily that would never die. Of course it was all the nutty part. The only reason they had ever been able to have a relationship was that although flashes of love and hate would fly up and spontaneously ignite them, he was the only one in her life who never said, *You sound insane.*

"It's a look," he said shrugging. Or he would have shrugged but her head was against his shoulder.

Her torso had begun to leak and swell. "Could my abdomen burst?" she asked. "Are there putrid gases building up?" There was a spot of bruisey yellow beneath her chin as if she were holding up a buttercup to see if she liked butter. But without the buttercup.

"Let's just keep driving. And then we'll find a place and get out and rest." He felt suddenly worried. "I won't mock you by doing things that you can't." This had been a complaint of hers when they were living together. He had never quite under-stood it.

"Oh, Finn. You don't see now? I am impossible to mock. For right this moment, I am unmockable. All my efforts at disguise will briefly prevail. For me. In my mind."

She swatted two blowflies away then opened the window so the breeze would take the fruit ones.

"OK," he said, not understanding. A dreamlike feeling had taken hold. Everything they passed they seemed to have passed before but not really. Perhaps God's continuity staff was on break. Occasionally it seemed they were just spiraling around, wearing mismatched clothes, hair parted on one side and then a moment later on the other with no wind or combing. They seemed generally to be passing the same sites over and over though nothing was exactly the same just mostly. Darkened fields with unreadable signs streaked by them on either side. The days, separate and named, seemed to be no longer arriving. He and Lily were between and among the hours and days rather than in them. The road ran on with its rough sections and moods and daft coordinates.

"Believe it or not the kind of tiredness I feel is not that different from the tiredness I felt when I was alive—"

"You're not alive?" He tried to arrange his face in mock surprise. What would happen to them being this long in each other's company? Could it manage to be the same company it always had been? Was she saying she had always been a little dead? Especially at the end of their relationship?

"You know what I mean—the kind of tiredness that sorrows your mind and pulls your head right down and you see that the pointlessness that spreads out before you has no path. Pointlessness has to have a path running through it, one that you can find and see, at least a little, or you are doomed." She paused. "Some animals don't make it through climate change."

He had always had difficulty with some of her monologues but tried hard to understand her. Moments of intense discovery are emotional for scientists, he had read recently. And a diamond achieved its shape through massive force. Did this apply to them? Perhaps they were alike in that their soliloquies were conducted in a lone spotlight on a stage. Like everyone's. Theater being the final retreat of the secretive. The houselights completely dark so who knew who was sitting out there, if anyone was at all.

"But why Jack of all people?" he asked now, startling himself. The name stabbed at him as ever. "Why?" He had brought the conversation down to a smudgier level.

"You're not being that nice to me," she said. She was fragrant. A whiff of truffle and marsh. It moved him.

"Forgive me," said Finn, "but as I drive along this highway, with trucks passing me, then me passing them, I've yet to achieve overview as to who we were to each other."

"We were each other to each other. Not everyone can say that."

"No. It's kind of a tongue twister." The part of her that avoided madness dragged in aspects of showmanship instead. There had always been something fraudulent in her happiness, and then she ignited the theatricality, even in unhappiness. "You were always performing," he added.

"What do you mean?"

"The clown shoes."

"The clown shoes are true. Very true."

"Why would they be true?"

"Because they are only shoes! They can't help what they are. They're just shoes."

"But your shoes even now are writing your lines."

"Writing my lines," she muttered then straightened and pulled away. She shuddered a little. "Why are you picking on my shoes?"

"Are you cold? Should I turn the heat up?"

"Lilies are heat-seeking. And sun-searching. Heliotropes. Did you not know that?"

"I didn't get that memo." He stared straight ahead at the gray road. "I got a different one." *One about water but do not overwater,* he did not say. Do not overwater the Lilies.

"I'm sorry that I failed you."

He nodded and swallowed. "Yes but—I'm sorry that I failed *you*."

"Well," she sighed. "Failure is how you meet people. Failure is how you sometimes get strong."

"You're talking from your clown shoes again."

"*Vesti la giubba,*" she said. "No more Rice Krispies."

He turned to glance at her while still trying to drive. "As you can see, I set out to find you but didn't really expect to succeed. I wasn't exactly prepared. No crackers. Plus? We are definitely out of Rice Krispies." But his suitcase from New York was helpfully in the back, beneath the cargo cover, and he believed it contained a small box of Wheaties.

Her silence was a mix of familiarity and apprehension.

He cleared his throat. "Are you ghosting me?" He supposed he was making a joke; no joke was beneath him. But in fact she had ghosted him many times in their years together. He responded by alternately ghosting her back and then sending begging texts. It was inconsistent and ineffective and very true to his own self: to thine own self be true.

They passed a large billboard that read GOD BLESS YOU, as if someone had sneezed. They crossed the Tennessee River once, then twice, were they about to cross it again? The river's turns were akin to a paperclip's. He had always admired paperclips, a twisted coupling made practical, and he often wondered who had invented them and whether the inventor had made a fortune.

"Where are we?" she asked.

"We're in a lull." The roadside that in spring would have been bejeweled with lupine and in summer with larkspur was now just half-dead approximate prairie and mountain pine. "Daylight savings time can be confusing."

Oh, that it were summer and they were walking along a path beneath the misty moon and listening to the happiness of little frogs which was like the happiness of cats, a vibrating purr, but louder, in groups, and under moist leaves. But no. They were in a chilly, chilly fall. And Lily was cold.

"About five hours from Knoxville, is my guess," he added. If he were going to be helpful he should be helpful.

"Good. I'm glad that's where we're going."

"I thought it was what you wanted."

"It is. You read my mind."

"I think you told me."

"You know? This is how our conversations always went. Right from the start. Even way back when, when you would try to get me out of bed while I slept off my sad little despairs."

"I remember it a little differently." He remembered after a while thinking, Why shouldn't she want to take her own life? She has already taken it. What is the point of carrying on the way she does—what is the meaning of that kind of life? Nothing.

"You do?"

"Yes I do." He didn't want to argue with her but there was always potential argument looming at every turn. What did Churchill say? *We shall fight on the beaches! We shall fight in the fields! We shall fight in the car.* "But maybe I'm wrong."

"Yes. Maybe you are."

Sad little despairs. "Can despair be plural like that?"

"Oh, my god, yes," she exclaimed.

He shook his head.

"Don't kill the messenger," she said.

S ister mine:

Spent the morning loosening the contents of a jammed drawer with a stick. It was like delivering a baby with makeshift forceps. Once the impediment got loose and the drawer was pried open there was nothing but old junk in there—letters, buttons, and bangle bracelets. I was looking for a hammer. Still I said, "Welcome to the world!" just in case anything popped out and also as a greeting to the junk.

Our board is served with flourish by Ofelia and me, or at least we imagine some style. Today we experimented with bare-bones gumbo. We put on those bangle bracelets and sang a Creole song. Still there is grumbling. What on God's earth are cabbage grits, and suchlike. We whistle "Turkey in the Straw" but there is mostly straw. June will bring us peaches from Georgia, I say, and there are grimaces and mouths pulled sidelong because June is a ways away. The handsome boarder often takes his evening meal elsewhere or perhaps not at all. I don't keep close tabs. Amidst the airy badinage at the meager nightly suppers I hear tell of rumors that in this very county the dead have risen as if it were Easter. There are also rumors of the vice versa, that people presumed to be living are not really or else have been seen lying in a ditch. Sometimes a warm ditch seems just the spot. Would you want to change places? You could write me to tell me yes or no, and I could read things over for errors in your reply. The afterlife overlays life in places like this because people have difficulty choosing between them. Eeny-meany. Miney-mo. I prefer the latter.

Early night.
Eliz.

They continued to drive. Through a storm that rose like a mountain range. Through the gray-edged pink of dawn. Along shantytowns of billboards and aerosolized frying oil when they passed a truck stop or a Dunkin' Donuts. They needed breakfast.

He could feel the grubby void of the universe coming for Lily, to lay claim again to its few pounds of loaned flesh. The soughing of her lungs matched the soughing of the car engine.

"Is there something you'd like to share with the class?" he asked her when she fell silent or seemed discouraged.

"Don't let me twist up like a pretzel," she said in a worried way. He could see her arms starting to do that. "Don't let anything do that to me."

Their car rides of the past—everyone needed moments of happiness recalled from different angles—the ones that stood out most in his memory, the summer ones with zithering crickets and the trilling notes of their own laughter, the steady speeding together into the aheadness, their quiet easy love, generated long ago from their pounding blood and bones and about which they had been so contented and indifferent, could not be recreated at this point. Now their love would descend upon them as a darkening screen, a veil of mourning.

Well, supposedly every galaxy had a black hole at its center. And when the technology got close you could hear the chirp. Every galaxy had a black hole and every black hole had a chirp, perhaps from the light it had captured forever and ever. The chirp was all that was left. It explained their car ride. It was their chirp.

"Let's pull over here and get something to eat." He had pulled into the parking lot of something called Parker's Pancakes.

"I don't want anything to eat," she said.

"Don't you have to use the ladies' room?"

She looked at him as if he were the most hopeless, foolish creature she had ever encountered. A look he recalled from their ostensible first date, when they were faux–fixed up by that heartless algorithm called "mutual friends" when in fact they had already met at that computer shop: it was a look he used to love a little bit, because you couldn't love it a lot.

"Ehn."

Their old melting together had now become her melting alone. Her complexion matched the sky, which currently resembled the gray-green yolk of an overcooked egg. One eye was closed and one was open, flashing a sequin made of light and water.

"Let me help you," he said, and he turned off the car and got out to open her door and lift her.

"You're going to carry me?" The smell of bacon blasted out through the air vent of the place.

"I sort of have to," he said, and he took her into Parker's Pancakes and just headed straightaway for the ladies' room, trudging through the truck stop part of it: the smell of popcorn, gleaming frankfurters, and pine disinfectant. They hobbled past the stacked cans of lighter fluid and Finn hoped nothing would ignite.

"What's going on?" asked the cashier.

"One of my legs fell asleep," said Lily, "and I can't wake it up."

"We won't be long," Finn called. He pointed at Lily. "She's my support clown."

"Fine," said the cashier. "The coast is clear."

There was no one else inside the restroom so Finn could go in with her. He leaned her against the sink, ran the faucet, wet a brown paper towel, and sudsed it up with soap. He wiped it along her face and neck and then used up all the paper towels that were left spot-rinsing and pat-drying her as best he could. She kept her eyes closed through the whole process and was still a tad damp but there were no more paper towels, just a hot-air hand dryer. He knew if she used that it would blow her skin right off, so he untucked and unbuttoned the shirt he was wearing and pressed it gently all over her. She leaned her cheek against his undershirt.

"You feel the same," she said.

"Fatter," he said.

"No."

"No? You think I've always been this fat?"

"You're not fat," she said, already bored by this subject. He lifted her up a little, to leave. "I'm sorry to be so perishable," she added.

"Yes, well."

"I'm a casserole of rot."

"Yum." He paused. "I mean that's kind of what all casseroles are."

"That's fair. I suppose. Cannibalism, I mean. It's very time-tested."

"You don't have to pee?" he asked. She just looked at him and sighed.

"Let's just go," she said. She started to shuffle out in her clown shoes.

"I'll carry you again," Finn said, buttoning his shirt.

She felt as light as balsa wood, and her shoes flopping around made her seem airborne. Her skin was sheer as organza.

On the road again, the sounds from each of them, their sighing and their breathing, were never in unison but came at staggered intervals forming a kind of round. The sun began setting mid-afternoon. The sky was backlit with galaxies that were momentarily close and bright.

"I fear I must stink," Lily said.

"You are simply classic and complex," he said.

"Yes, thank you. And room temperature."

"Lush and ripe and well integrated."

"Hmmmm."

"You have the mixed bouquet of jasmine, tobacco, dried apple blossoms, plus rose, lilac, and raisin. Some tannins. There are always tannins."

"Why *is* that."

"A certain acidity to offset the sugar, as well as the good body, underneath which percolates the Proustian potpourri of a 1970s spice rack, some stale oregano and flowering thyme, scarcely scented."

"I don't like it when time flowers. Showy." She eyed her arms skeptically. Beneath her skin there was the wiggling look of maggots in meat. Levity versus gravity was not a fair fight.

"Nonetheless? Brings a long finish. A very long finish. With some dusty earth and spicy oak and just a hint of cereal. Some Grape-Nuts, I think, and some pasta primavera. Perhaps a dash of refrigerator vegetable drawer. An old carrot. A roasted avocado."

"You shouldn't roast avocados."

"That's what I mean. I'm trying to warn you." He thought he might be able to itemize an amusing sachet for miles along these roads but had already plunged his recitation into the compost.

"Sorry," she said.

He turned himself over to thoughts of the day of her demise. He wasn't sure how he felt about drowned people. Or even half-drowned people. Whichever it was.

"Can one *be* dead?" she asked now.

"What do you mean?"

"I mean if you are *being,* how are you also dead?"

"I think I missed that long-ago class on linking verbs."

"No, you probably didn't," she said. "You just don't want to say."

She moved in and out of napping again. The whirring about he had once felt emanating from within her had vanished. He felt it instead within himself. It took the form of pressured speech, an electric movement of the limbs, some blinking.

She stirred. "Once the flower is pollinated it doesn't last as long," she said.

"Are you pollinated? You didn't tell me!"

"I'm a lot of things I didn't tell you."

"Because you knew I knew."

"Maybe," she said with her eyes closed.

"I'm glad we're not talking about Jack," he said provocatively.

"Yes," she said.

He pressed his foot down on the accelerator. Now evening scenery was breaking over them from the front and rushing by on the sides—rushed like quickly assembled scenery for a play, the now starless sky a charcoal foam. The car sped forward. Glued to the windshield, in the form of the rearview mirror, was a little landscape painting of the very recent past. The car seemed to want to fly. It would be the pale horse and Lily the pale rider.

Daylight was starting to return in briefly florid streaks.

From his peripheral vision he believed Lily looked at him with love. He was quite sure it was love. "My heart is in my mouth," she said. "I mean literally."

Occasionally they would find themselves poking along behind a truck—an eighteen-wheeler on the interstate, a tractor on the county pikes. A four-by-four full of two-by-fours anywhere at all. The slow pace would stall out his brain and the meandering conversations of car trips—how many cold cases do you think there are in that town; is pubic waxing an accommodation to hard-wired pedophilia; look at that deserted little church—would drift off and he would revisit his own injuries and complaints.

Staring straight ahead at some cows in a cattle hauler, he said, "You were willing to take all those memories of us, the memory of me—you who knew me like nobody else!—and you were willing to kill the me that was dependent on you for staying alive."

"Yes. You," Lily said with a sigh. "I guess it's about you."

"It *includes* me," he said. The sky now had the low dark fat of withheld snow.

"Yes, it seems to." He glanced sideways at her. She refused to glance back at him. "Life is a tough room," she said. He wanted to slam on the brakes, jump out of the car, rip a wiper off the windshield, and stab himself in the eye. Eye stabbing was a recurrent desire he had to manage. So instead of slamming on the brakes, he passed the truck ahead of him in a dangerous roar, settling in front of it but not slowing down, watching the vehicle shrink in the side mirror.

Perhaps they could sing in the car, she asked. And she began:

> *The boughs are breaking*
> *The house is quaking*
> *Now there's heartaching*
> *All over the ground*
>
> *What should I've done*
> *Walked instead of run?*
> *It's raining through the sun*
> *All over the ground*
>
> *Our blasted past went fast*
> *unlike the fleeting now*
> *I give you*
> *the crooked broken bough*
> *Shave and a haircut: two bits.*

"Not a happy song," she added. She rubbed the roots of her hair until they had the nice grassy smell of a freshly killed stinkbug. Her legs in his corduroy pants looked like celery sticks. He had always accepted every incarnation of her. Her starved self. Her shadow self.

"Most songs aren't. Well, a lot aren't," he added. "I don't know the percentage."

" 'Happy Birthday' is happy—especially on any day that's not actually your birthday. Have you ever noticed that to sing harmony you have to go above or below the melody but proceed exactly like the melody, as if you were the melody, as if your part were the main idea? You have to proceed confidently with delusion." Like love. Harmony was hard.

"Ever the way I suppose where music is concerned. Yet where would we be without music."

"Two of our mass shooters were named Dylan. Music is worthless," she declared.

He would have to stop for gas before too long.

And when he did, standing there at the self-serve island, the wind whipped his sparse hair flat against his head. The cold air was like menthol and the fog of his breath like Salems smoked in memory, at another time. When he got back in the car Lily was asleep, and he made his way to the ramp and got on the interstate going south.

The drive was full of scattered flurries that vanished, and the sky lost and gained a look of dirty ice. Somewhere well past the bridge over the Ohio, rolling on into the hills of Kentucky or was it Tennessee—one of those states lying on its side in defeat, slotted in like slate in a stacked-stone fence—he pulled off at an exit that was showing lodging down the road—4 MILES—

and when he arrived it was a double-verandaed something called
The Jumping Rest Tourist Lodge Home, an old inn perched on
a hill between the turnpike and a creek. On one side of the
house was an old privy and on the other an old metal hand
pump for water. Finn pulled in, got out, and opened the passenger's side door. The engine going quiet had woken her. When
she slept she could go still as a picture, then life would steal back
into her and she would whir again. When she awoke she would
gasp, as if pinched.

"Where are we?"

"We're on the corner of Garrison Turnpike and South
Sunken Road."

Now she was pawing through the glove compartment. "Do
you have sunglasses in here? I think I should wear sunglasses."
She pulled out some crooked green aviator glasses. "Oh look!"
She put them on.

"A cross between Janis Joplin and a state trooper. Hang on,
I'm going to sweep you off your feet," he said and scooped her
up in his arms.

"I do like the sound of that but really: I can walk," she said,
twisting free.

"Lean against me," he replied, and with Finn half-carrying
her up the hill they walked toward the door of The Jumping Rest
Tourist Lodge Home, which had a light that said OFFICE and
another light that said less certainly PEN. He propped her against
the porch wall and then went back and got his suitcase from
the car. The nearby creek appeared to run into a dammed-up
pond and he thought he heard the contralto kazoos of the swans
again, the faint adjustments of their wings, resettled like shawls
for warmth. He and Lily had not outpaced the flock.

"No buzzards, right?" she asked. Trees jutted their bare branches into the sky in expressions of fright or surprise or warning or why choose.

"No," he said.

The decrepit manse was an old Queen Anne heap. Out back was a brook that ran into a bog and then a ravel of sunflowers. On the stairs were pots of tansy and chrysanthemums. He stepped up on the side veranda and without lifting the brass knocker on the yellow door just went in, carrying Lily then setting her down inside, where she stood holding his arm.

"This house is kinda janky," said Lily. "We're sleeping here?"

"You have a better idea?" OK, there would be fuzz on the furniture. But she was in no position to protest dust or mold.

"Faute de mieux," she said.

Death had improved her French. She whacked him lightly on the arm. *"C'est bien, n'est-ce pas?"* Green wainscoting anchored the room and above it was wallpaper with golden flocked fleurs-de-lis. Around on the walls hung painted bird plates: partridges and grouse. "I like the yellow *mais peut-être* not the *fleurs*. Didn't I used to have a vest like this?" Lily asked.

"As part of your costume?"

"Yes." The time in the car had made them aspects of one another, a feature and fatality of car trips and love. He grabbed the bag from the porch.

"What can I do for y'all?" asked a woman, rising from her chair. Her desktop sign read NO SICK PEOPLE. She wore a lilac sweater and her hair was the velvety gray of hearth ash. But underneath the sweater Finn could see she was dressed in fancy black, lacy like a spider or a merry Italian widow or an unhappy mother of the bride. Her face was plaited with creases.

"We need a room," said Finn.

"I'm in ongoing work-around here," said the innkeeper, flipping open her laptop. She didn't look that busy. In fact, the whole place looked empty. If she said, "I'll see what I can rustle up," or spoke of her herbal medicines he would know this was an episode of Sunday night television. But Lily spoke first.

"Sorry if I resemble a swamp person." She had kept her sunglasses on.

"We're no strangers to swamp people," said the innkeeper, wiping her hands on her apron. "A lot of characters have stepped in here through the many decades. Jesse James, they say. A lot of history, a lot of other infamous rebels and other fugitives I can tell you about if you want to know more—"

"That's OK. We're good," said Lily.

The innkeeper pursed her lips. "Sheets are clean. And we don't steal your jewelry while you sleep. There's hot water. Though I'd appreciate it if y'all didn't drain it completely."

What they needed was to shine themselves up a bit, a little rinse. "Just a little rinse," said Finn.

"Pardon our dust," said piebald Lily. She was starting to look like death's junk drawer. He pulled her closer.

"We're really not as sketchy as we appear," added Finn. Lily needed basting or debasting—he wasn't sure. There was the mild smell of week-old poultry coming off her.

Lily looked at her own hands then peered into his eyes and whispered, "Am I too—dunno. Translucent? Or have I oxidized?"

Everything except her nails did look a little clear, like certain Amazon frogs or the Pompidou museum, the inner workings showing; thank god for the French, who had given Lily a few phrases and the look of art, suggesting Very Out of Town.

The innkeeper studied them, and Finn could see perhaps how Lily seemed to others—was the bruising simply *moulage*? Were the shoes an act? Might they be in an experiment together or perhaps a traveling circus? Was the translucence a trick? Was this a mohair jellyfish and her gamekeeper? "Mmmmmm," said the innkeeper. She opened a drawer and drew up some paper-work. She swiped Finn's Visa in a plastic flatbed imprinter. Few electronics here but for the laptop.

"What is the name of this town?" asked Finn.

"Tyler," said the innkeeper.

"After the president?"

"No. The town used to be called Turkeytail but then changed its name. Tyler was not the president. He was a drunk who won the card game, so he got to name the town."

She swiped the Visa card again and stared down, then handed the card back to Finn. "That dog won't hunt. You got another card? Or we do take cash. Also gold, silver, bitcoin, and bitcoin cash."

"Let me see." Finn handed her another.

She slid it through then waited before saying, "Y'all good," and handing it back. "If y'all could sign the guest book I'd greatly appreciate it."

"What's happening?" murmured Lily, her breath like gaso-line.

Wind roared stormily around the house, rushing into the window sashes, transforming them briefly into flutes.

"Kind of like a recital room," said the innkeeper.

A version of "Für Elise" almost filled the air. Though it was probably "Turkey in the Straw."

As if on cue two musicians came in the door. Their hands held the hourglass shapes of black guitar cases, as if they were carrying their own shadows. They nodded and headed up the stairs to their rooms. Perhaps there would be music later.

"This place has been in the family for a long time. A lot of faded dreams." She smiled. "Not all of which are mine. Some? I'm simply descended from." She smiled again. "It's not haunted or anything," she said. "It's a house of good repute. I don't keep the shotgun loaded."

"Should you?"

She ignored him. "I've given you the best room though it's patched," she said. "It's got some history. The windows have some stained-glass panes—you might see in one of them the old surgeon who used to cut off the soldiers' legs on the veranda. Also, I patched the wallpaper with scraps from the presidential box, when they were selling those after they tore the theater in Washington down. I suppose as souvenirs they can go both ways, but we here are fans of Mr. Lincoln."

"Who isn't," said Finn, and the woman raised her thick, still-dark eyebrows, as if to say, *I wouldn't holler that.*

"Not naming names," she said then changed the subject. "This place once aspired to be a high cotton boardinghouse, if one can say such a thing. A piano in the parlor and whatnot. Just plumped all the pillows to get the bugs out of them." She gave him her Splenda smile. "There's two ginger cats downstairs here, Red and Les, but they keep to theirselves. Red and Less Red. What else can you name cats."

"I once had one named Hercules," said Finn. "And one named Quiche."

"For cats?" said the landlady.

"'Fraid so."

Now she was just going to ignore him on the subject of cat names. "If anything upstairs seems not to work, just kick it, smack it, or unplug it then plug it back in. We're on the zig and zag of the Mason-Dixon Line here and it's just how things are. We don't mind but sometimes the guests do. Also? There was a tornado ripped through here last week so I'm also housing two live human orphans but they are very quiet and on the first floor. They are named Meghan and Lee. Meghan's good people but very sad. Can't tell about Lee." She paused pensively. "There's breakfast down here in the morning until ten. We used to be known for our decadent brunches but things have gotten more spare." She cleared her throat as if apologizing. "I have a wood-pecker every morning up there on the left soffit. Hope he doesn't bother you. The cats of course are no good where woodpeckers are concerned. And I've tried the peppermint, the foil streamers, the wind chimes, and the fake painted owls. I've now sent away for a have-no-heart trap. I'm not sentimental. It's no life for a creature of God, banging your beak into wood."

"No it's not," agreed Lily.

"And it's not even for food. It's to impress the females. A mating ritual! Better just to have it all end so the poor thing can start over again as some other species entirely."

Their room upstairs was dank as a church and smelled of old wallpaper paste. A large seashell propped the door open. There was no lock or key. Braided rugs were scattered about the wide boards of the maple floors. The bathroom and bedroom windows were patched with ambrotypes serving as make-do stained glass. Finn had heard this was sometimes done with old photography plates when windows broke and there was noth-ing else. It was a beautiful hack, and in these various portraits the stiff, seated, injured, amputated people in their reverse black and white seemed to blink with interest when the sinking sun shifted behind them. But their dour faces, even in their flipped-about black and white, made him feel sorry for them. Despite his skepticism about contemporary times, not one person he ever saw depicted from the past looked happy. They seemed to gaze out of their pictures with a deep wish for time travel and resurrection. Their stares said, *Stay where you are. It's better where you are. I would like to be there. Whatever your concerns are? let's trade.*

Memories from another time and other people and in the form of humidity saturated the place. Any given time always had other times beneath it. If he were more of a psychic he felt he might access them, and confessional tales would ensue, after which he and Lily would just have to dry and disinfect the whole place by setting it on fire.

The bathroom had a table fan and Finn tested it out. Like every southern motor he'd ever encountered it was old and choral, with an extra whir, plus a buzz. He turned it back off.

The tub was in the main room, against the wall, perpendicular to the bed. It was encased in wood, something he'd never seen before, and some worn stencils had been painted onto the sides. The wood surround made it easier to sit on its edge. He put the rubber stopper in the drain and ran the hot water, swirling it around until the water became the perfect warmth. He stood. "Come here," he said to Lily, and cradling the dense sweet rot of her against his chest he slipped her into the tub with all her clothes and wrappings, though not her shoes, which he had already pulled off and set in the corner near the window. Once she was in the tub he cut all the clothes away from her, including his own corduroys, with some scissors in the shaving kit he kept in his bag, and he pulled the shirt and the trousers out of the tub and tossed them in a rubbish bin. He had additional clothes that she could wear. He washed her carefully with one of the washcloths the inn had provided. "Thank you," she murmured. "Thank you. Thank you." Her body was both strange and familiar, her breasts parabolas of blue and brown, and when the evening light shifted outside her ashy skin seemed to have a phosphorescence to it. Her torso was mottled but also creamy in places like a New Age candle, and he pressed his lips to the closest part of her branching collarbones. A small remembering smile appeared on her face but she did not look at him. When he pressed his hand gently to her upper arm it left a pink print.

He opened a small bottle of shower gel he'd found on the bureau. It had a Hilton label and a spicy geranium scent like aftershave and with it he sudsed the odor of fish and cheese off her, then ran some water into a pitcher and poured it over her head, watching it rain down her face, mixing with her own spittle. Her eyes closed and her mouth widened into a tragedian's grimaced sorrow but there was no other motion, no movement of the shoulders to indicate a sob. Now would be the time to cry, however. Now would be the time to let her silently rain tears out of her cracking head: this was what eyes were for. This was what a bath was for. Perhaps the feeling of water was reminding her of what she had done. He took a washcloth and gently moved it around her body, her skin slipping slightly. Sloughage rolled off her into the bathwater forming a brown film. When he moved the washcloth down one arm the skin of her hand, soaking in the water, seemed to come off a bit and he slipped it back on like a glove. She was now sheer as the rice wrap on a spring roll, the bean sprouts and chopped purple cabbage visible inside her.

He continued to rub more gel into her scalp, which moved loosely around on her skull. He mashed the lather into her hair and then refilled the pitcher and poured it over her again. This time the water was cooler and it seemed to wake her up.

"I am a fish," she said.

"You are a fish. Or fishlike."

"My mother is a fish."

"Yup. There is that."

"I suppose by now I have violated the three-day fish rule."

"The fish rule does not apply to you."

"That is the nicest thing anyone has ever said to me."

When he thought he had done the best he could, he lifted her up and swaddled her in two white towels, which would have to serve as a kind of rinsing as well.

A small writing desk had been placed next to the tub, perhaps as a kind of vanity. A gilt-framed mirror full of spots from where the silver had worn off hung above it on the wall for reference, and in its reflection, surrounded by wallpaper of light blue roses, patched with a square of pink leaves and blooms from the presidential theater box wallpaper (if the label pasted next to it was to be believed), emerging from this palimpsest of floral paper, was a hologram of a very tired Lily. He began drying her with the towels when suddenly she brightened and said, "I have to pee! Can you help me to the commode?"

Was there no greater sign of life than having to pee?

Once there, she tilted then flopped forward, her hair still twisted and wrapped in a towel. "I used to watch myself pee this way. Just peek through the space between the toilet seat and the rim of the bowl and watch the rain and the dark bombs and boulders. World War Three."

The window near the commode was patched with ambrotypes, and one was placed with its ruby side in so that the starchy woman portrayed could look out into the world as her true self. But the ruby side, reflecting the ceiling light, pinkened the room. A sunset. Next to the starchy woman was a brooding lass.

There was a trickle into the toilet water.

Lily clutched at some toilet paper and then proceeded to wipe herself everywhere starting with her forehead, her skin pale as tallow, her eyes gold as chicken fat, her expression and complexion a swirling, vibrating mother-of-pearl.

"I'm done," she said.

"I have an extra shirt you can wear."

"Thank you," she said. "I always loved your shirts."

"You need a lot of them, as a teacher. And then you can't get new ones because you're a teacher on a teacher's salary. So they grow soft." He paused. "And then you lose your job."

"And you give them to me! They do something for me. They add charm, I'm sure. I guess my charisma has always been a bit ramshackle. In need of a susceptible imagination . . ."

"Maybe." She smiled as he awkwardly put a white shirt on her. It looked like pajamas. But everything on her now looked like pajamas. "Shall we go to bed? Are you tired?"

He helped her toward the bed and pulled back the linens and quilt. The mattress beneath was wavy old, and together they gerrymandered themselves into its hidden curves and valleys. He pressed the fronts of his knees into the backs of her knees. Lily sighed. "Everything is too much," she said.

"Yes," he said. He understood that their clock was ticking, that he was likely to lose her yet again, perhaps this time to evaporation. But lying close he could feel the throb, treble, and woof of her pulse and nervous system.

"And yet?" she said. "Here with you? This is my home." He discerned the throat-tug of a key change in a song. But nothing was Lily's home, though he did not say this. It was not her fault that her sudden hectic love was always like that—a flash mob that emerged from nowhere, a dance that twisted out of anonymous movements, then receded back into the crowd, which was sometimes shouting "The whole world is watching" and sometimes "Free Barabbas."

"The dead prefer the company of the living," she added. "Better light banter."

"What is the light banter of the dead like?"

"Don't get me started. You don't want to know. Or maybe you've had a taste." She then began to sing. *"Oh, how lovely is the evening, is the evening."* And he joined her in the round, which years ago they used to sing to get themselves to sleep. Perhaps it would work again.

"When the bells are sweetly ringing, sweetly ringing."

"Ding, dong, ding, dong."

He kissed her head.

"Do we have a safe word?" she asked.

"They're all safe."

"No. They're all dangerous. Do you remember this song? *In my cerise chemise all full of fleas / I cross my legs and scratch my knees / Can you rub my back oh please . . . "*

"I could," he said.

"It's just a song," she said.

He felt her skin sliding, and further lodged his knees into the backs of hers. He thought their makeshift joy could, if asked to, live forever in this room like a warming fire.

She began to make a nickering sound in her sleep and then to snore. Or was it his own snoring? As he closed his eyes and fell away into the back spaces of his head, he was not sure where the sounds came from; perhaps once more he and Lily were in concert. Her teeth began to snap and grind. *Shhhhhh,* he breathed into her dark soft ear and she went quiet. Perhaps pretending to be dead! Surprise! Ha! Ha! Was this not proof that living was funny? He tried very hard not to think about all the ways they had failed each other. He could not sleep deeply; his arm was around her but it felt like he had dislocated his shoulder. All his bones felt out of joint, so he slid out and got up. On the floor was a chamber pot full of fake flowers. He nudged it out of the way with one bare foot and wandered over to a bookcase, a heavy knickknack area in most houses but here were some actual books. He turned on a lamp and studied them for something he could bring to the nearby reading table to read. Nothing seemed to have been dusted or rearranged for a long time. He saw a spider and moved to kill it but it darted too quickly: one minute it had appeared stuck in its corner and then suddenly it bounded with great speed and vanished into space. He looked at the book spines again. They were mostly titleless volumes, perhaps personal things that had been bound at a bindery, though there was a Bible, a guide to butterflies, some Dickens, one *Uncle Tom's Cabin,* and various confessions and histories of Civil War battles. He pulled out the guide to butterflies. Butterflies were ghosts, it said. The earthly creature was the caterpillar. The butterfly the spirit. He felt he knew this already—of course butterflies were ghosts!—and replaced the book in favor of a brittle, faded red one with a cracked spine and tawny, deckled pages. Inside was a woman's journal all handwritten in the form of letters. He flipped through and saw that they went on for some time, almost a year, and that they were written to a particular person, a sister, but obviously never mailed. Unless they were bound here as copies. He began to read.

Are you really up there? Can you hear me? Or are you with us down here?

Darling sister,

There is much strangeness to report. Perhaps I just do not really understand who people are, myself included. Is that the surprise the Lord has in store for us? Surprise! Look at who y'all are!

The handsome boarder Jack has for a while now increased his bothering of Ofelia. I don't care for the nature of his friendliness to her, it is narrowed, performed as to an object. He can be expansive with the other lodgers, and when he first arrived to my full house way back when and slept in his tent out back he played the gentleman to perfection, even from the tent. One night I lay in it with him speaking of all manner of matters of the heart, and that was my mistake. Now he takes liberties everywhere. But Ofelia has it worse.

"Miss Libby!" she will plead and edge toward me. "Help," she whispers.

"Don't bother her!" I say to him when I come upon this because she is too shy to do so herself and cautious. She will cast a worried glance my way when I see that he has seemed to corner her in a room for a conversation. If she can scurry off, she scurries.

Late evening, after she has gone home, on the nights she goes home, he comes to me to speak of the colored and their ways.

"Why, I have no idea what you are talking about," I say. "And lest you think otherwise, there's no cause for you to describe Ofelia to me. I think she and I have shared our lives quite a bit. Don't attempt to stranger-splain her: she is my friend. And you leave her be."

"Hoo-ee. Aren't we the aging abolitionist."

"Yessir, we just might be." Repeatedly I must send him away, mostly with success but once he lingered. I was filled with a new loathing. "Might I add? The abolition hath already occurred."

Then one evening, ringing the little bell I keep strung in the upstairs hall, he summoned me to his room complaining of illness. He was in bed wearing long johns and a short top hat. This self-contradictory costume did not surprise me.

"Miss Libby, I fear I am ill," he said, with a slight smile.

"I fear I'm not a nurse," I explained, "but only an innkeeper. There is a sign in the window which you might have attended to: NO SICK PEOPLE. We don't want to turn this into a sanitorium. But I will bring you some tea." Which I did. Though I took my time brewing it and by the time I brought it upstairs to him he appeared to have fallen asleep beneath the covers. I set it on the nightstand near his bed, and after I did he stirred to clutch my wrist and brought it up to his thick mustache.

"I want to smell your perfume," he said.

"I don't think it's the healing sort," I said. It was a French hand lotion full of rose, and surely it had dissipated hours before. "It's devilwood and drupe," I said.

He held my hand with one hand and petted it with his other. I pulled mine away and stepped backward and the force of it almost caused me to fall.

"This is not a brothel," I said.

"What a shocking thing to say," replied Jack.

"There's your tea," I said. I nodded at the cup and tried to leave.

"This is very civilized and I thank you. There is a matter I wanted to raise."

"A matter?"

"You have a scarecrow in the backyard?"

"Yes, I have a kitchen garden and can't have the crows eating the seed."

"And the scarecrow is dressed in a Union soldier's uniform?" I became briefly still, watching him speak. "Is that to scare away the seceshers?"

"The rebs? For them I have some tansy and a ravel of sunflowers that get knocked over easily. It gives them a fright."

"Why Miss Libby, you've been eating too many of your own butter beans." He smiled.

"Someone has to," I said. I hadn't known until then that they might have a reputation.

"Federal blue on a scarecrow? That can be interpreted different ways."

"Many hapless rebs were dressed in blue. For some that was all they had, from before the war," I informed him. "They were often shot mistakenly by their own men." I was biting my lips and tongue and everything else in my mouth as if it were soft meat. "Furthermore? You may recall that toward the end of the fighting the gray uniforms did not make it out this far. Transport issues. North Carolina was the problem, I believe. Is there any other matter before I say good-night."

"Well, yes, ma'am. There is."

"All right then."

"You don't think Ofelia is too savage for your house?" He drank from the lemon balm tea in a long draining inhalation.

I told him I thought no such thing and that he had no business speaking a single word against her. As I was turning again to leave he asked me if it might be possible to have more tea. "It's quite good," he said.

I said I thought yes it would be possible.

"Don't tarry," he said with an inscrutable wink, and I took the cup from him and went downstairs. I don't know quite what came over me next. But I made the tea very strong. If you know what I mean. I think you know what I mean. If you think of father when he was ill at the very end, and you and I making the tea with mother, I know you will know what I mean.

When I returned upstairs with my lantern and the tea, he was naked and in the tub but there was no water. The tub tray hid the family jewels. His chest was dark with hair. Candles were lit around the room. His cork foot with its sashes and straps lay at the side of the tub with his shoe still on it.

"Should I bathe in the tea?" he asked.

"I don't quite care what you do." It was too late for me to bring him water for a bath. I would not pump water at night. I set the lamp on the writing table and the cup on the tub tray.

He stuck his pinky in the tea and dabbed a little behind each ear. He grinned and drank it all down once more. I was backing away.

"Come here," he said.

"I'll take the cup is all." I put it on the table.

"Is that all?" I imagined he was used to brothels and now half-believed this was one.

I pulled up a chair, watching him grow drowsy in the tub and slide down a bit.

"Do I make you happy, Libby?" he was murmuring. "Because I want to more than anything. Every time I declaim my memorized Elizabethan poetry I think of you."

Instead of answering I launched into a diagonal direction, conversation-wise.

"I will tell you a story that has some bearing," I said. "Six years ago I had a bunch of Union soldiers here, boys, just boys. Young and no trouble at all. Not at all. They were happy that the war appeared over. A telegram had said that it was. And they came downstairs on Easter Sunday and sat down to breakfast only to learn that the President had been shot in the back of the head. In a theater. The President who had been their idol and their inspiration. Well, they pushed back their chairs and sobbed into their biscuits. Inconsolable boys sobbing and heaving on Easter. It was a piercing thing. I will never forget it."

Then I leaned in and slammed the tub tray hard against his throat so there was no scream, just the eyes cracked aflame like kindling, bright with moving blood.

I quickly stood and put my very own chair cushion over his face and pressed hard. "I am done with you," I said. And in less than five minutes sure enough I was. "People don't think I know who they are," I added. "That is a sorrowful mistake." There was not that much thrashing of the one foot. Some flailing of the arms I had to dodge. There was no time for him to call me something Elizabethan, such as a dissembling harlot or a scurvy canker blossom. I was a one-woman sting operation. A wild-flower into sticky business to trap a fly. I was an asphodel that is actually a carnivore. I was God only knows.

But I had stunned myself and grabbed the lamp and quickly left the room, locking the door behind me.

In the morning bringing a breakfast tray with not much on it I pretended to discover him there like that, and Ofelia and I cried out together Lord have mercy. I sent her down to the sheriff's office to impart word of it. I oughtn't have sent her. It was cowardly of me not to go myself. But I no longer knew quite who I was. Though that lasted but a morning. Still, it is seldom the perpetrator's job to report the death. Though I suppose sometimes it is occasionally done, but my mind casts about and lands only on our President whose killing was quickly announced from the stage, in delusional Latin, they say, right after a very loud laugh from the crowd. Though others who were at the horror show say: no there was not a word of Latin. The Latin was invented afterward to gussy up their cause. The murderer was too busy trying to hobble away and escape as fast as he could. That surely is the truth.

Love you like chickens,
Eliz.

"I don't want breakfast," said Lily. "But I do want this nice white bathrobe they're selling."

"I think they're not really for sale. It seems to be a paper robe."

"Even better."

The woodpecker was starting up outside. Grackles ascended in a scatter with their weird groupthink, swirling.

"I see you liked the bathrobe," said the innkeeper. Why was Lily wearing it? Did she have to actually wear it? Beneath it she had on another one of Finn's white shirts. It was a warm Indian summer day. The innkeeper came out from behind her desk. "I've wrapped up some scones for your trip. You ought to take those. Also some chicken-fried fried chicken. I had extra. Our breakfasts as I think I mentioned used to be quite decadent, but that was years ago."

"Thank you," said Lily. The paper robe was like a floating white cocoon around her.

"A toast to the bride," said the innkeeper, lifting her coffee cup.

"Thanks," said Lily, who had never been married and never would be.

"Yes, thank you," said Finn. He had stolen the notebook from the room, slid it into the back waistband of his pants with his jacket covering it, but his plan was to return the thing eventually.

The morning light was lemony and bright. "The sun so hot I froze to death," said Lily. A dark spackle of high migrating birds briefly decorated the sky. "Those buzzards, you think?"

"No." He craned his neck to look at a chevron of ducks. "Buzzards circle."

"Yes, that's right. Like a lasso."

In the car she pulled down the car visor then opened the bag of scones and chicken. Taking a cranberry from one of the scones, she rubbed it on her lips and cheeks for a rosy tinge. "Instantaneous health," she exclaimed, looking in the mirror. Then she took a raisin and filled in her eyebrows. No longer a fruit tree, she seemed a sweet and putrid gouache.

To remain both distracted and focused while driving, Finn was running through the titles of books he'd read in college and trying to recall their authors. "Who wrote *Seven Types of Ambiguity*?" Finn asked.

"Snow White."

"Who wrote *The Collected Works of Voltaire*? Everyone thinks it's Voltaire."

"A sucker born every minute."

"What do the P and the T stand for in Barnum?"

"Pass and The. Simple table manners."

"Who wrote *Uncle Tom's Cabin*?"

"Oh, man, I always forget that one. I've gotta stop sleeping in the park fountain."

"Who wrote *Song of Bernadette*?"

"Bernadette."

"You have a lot of weird knowledge."

"You're always putting me in your classes and making me take your tests."

"I don't give that many tests."

"No?"

"Don't believe in them."

"What do you mean? That's what school is. That's what life is. Test after test," she said.

"But what do tests measure?" He got on his pedagogical hobbyhorse, of which he had a full stable. "They measure: Do you have a quiet home with reliable Wi-Fi?"

"No. I'm living in a car right now."

"Did you sleep well last night?"

"No, I really did not."

"Can you concentrate?"

"On what?"

"Are you forced to hold down a part-time job? Do you organize your time efficiently?"

"That was always a problem."

"Are you in a gang?"

"Depends how you look at it."

"Do you take performance-enhancing drugs such as SAT prep courses?"

"Used to. Meant to. Tried Sudafed once. With coffee. I think."

"Do you have private tutors? Did you go to math camp? How well do you cheat?"

Lily fell still. "Pretty well," she said. Then she added, "No, I don't cheat well, really."

"No," Finn said, his eyes on the road. "You don't."

Sometimes vehicles glided past them, old retired couples speeding up for a dangerous thrill, and Finn wished they would take him too, wherever they were going. But they were going way past where he was going. His GPS was directing and his signal to turn right was on already.

"I'm looking in the side-view mirror," she said.

"What do you see?"

"A winding road disappearing into haze."

"I fear there's more of that ahead."

"I have no plans," said Lily.

Finn glanced over at her. Her watery eyes suddenly now seemed bugged out and fiery. "What do you mean you have no plans? Of course you have plans." She was perhaps as ambivalent as he was.

"I just read my palm and now that it has no dirt on it?" She flashed it quickly in his peripheral vision. "Nada. Fate has changed."

She seemed always to have something up her sleeve. Perhaps he could talk her into life.

"Remember when we first met?" Lily asked and of course he did. In the computer repair shop run by young people and strewn with so many electronic parts it looked like a robot war. He had been there for an upgrade. She had been there to sell them her old iPod.

"It's practically the only lawful place that people can meet now—in real life," Finn said.

"Was that real life?"

"Be nice," he said.

"When we met, I said, 'Let us entangle and embroil,' and you said, 'Yeah, right.'"

The repair shop, the curbside parking, the exchange of numbers, then at her suggestion—"You were somewhat suggestive," he said now—he arranged for her to visit the school on Career Choices day to speak about the sick and how one tries to make them laugh and think life is good despite everything. Dressed as a clown. But before he could tell her again—for she used to like to hear it over and over, how he had loved her almost instantly, though he could never reach the top or bottom of her infinite self, or so it had seemed, not just now but even at the start—he fell into a new fugue and rush of memory. Her presence had always been alternative, somewhat like a set of choices, none of them wrong, none of them correct: her choice, his choice, the clown school's choice. She had then invited him over to look at her rotted deck, since he had stupidly boasted of carpentry skills and having painted his house three times. "Look at this rot! How will you ever land a man with a deck like this?" Finn had said to her as they stood on her decayed and moss-edged boards. She had smiled back so he continued. "Dressing up like a clown for a living and with a deck like that? I guess you don't really want a man."

Her face had gone still and the silence between them felt a little endless until she'd said, "I guess I don't."

He had always been helpless before her. His life became a halting imitation of personal choice. He was like a lost planet orbiting a chilly red dwarf star instead of an actual sun. She mentioned doing a Planned Parenthood fundraiser, and said to him, "Everyone speaks of the abortion rights of the mother, but how about the abortion rights of the baby? The unwanted baby has a right to an abortion as well!" He only now recognized so many things as signs. When they first slept together he turned to her in the morning and said, "I know this is too soon, but I do believe I love you." She had said nothing, though he waited for a long time until at last he added, "I know you really love me, too," and she had said, "So what?"

Now on their way to the end they switched parts. "I know you really love me," she said, studying his profile. They had passed mountains and valleys filled with milky fog, and rivers with alarmingly rusty bridges. The road was an unfurling ribbon without a gift.

"So what?" he replied, staring at the road. She turned and just looked out the window, the gray and yellow of the countryside flying steadily by.

"Hindsight is fifty-fifty," she said with a sigh, as if making a lighthearted but sweeping gesture to the chaos of their past. "I guess that's a joke. Does it work?"

"You're the professional."

"Well. I mostly do sight gags. As you often remind me." She kept her gaze out the window. "Do you ever hate every single thing you see?"

At first he said nothing. "No," he said finally.

She nodded a little. "You're very lucky. Do you ever feel the smell of freshly cut grass is a cry for help from the grass?"

"Maybe." He was failing at keeping her alive. Driving her to her death a second time. Or perhaps this counted as a third. Regardless: it was yet again. Perhaps he was simply a killer.

"Remember my unicycle?"

"How could I forget?"

"I had just learned to ride it. I was really trying to learn—children's comedy is not just pratfalls and hiccup jokes and passing gas, though that one always works—but I was retarded."

"You can't say *retarded* anymore," he chided her. How many

faculty meetings had there been over the years where this had been discussed?

"I know, but *I really* was." She paused. "That's the thing about death," she said. "You get to say whatever you want."

"It's a safe space?"

She nodded vaguely. "It's a safe space for me."

But not for the learning disabled, he did not say. Instead he asked, "Do you ever think that everyone's relationship with everyone else is an invention? But sometimes you get other people to participate in the invention along with you?"

"Inventions are good. Hey, the lightbulb was an invention! And look what happened. Lots of lightbulb jokes. I love lightbulb jokes. Even though I can't think of any right now offhand. It's tough when no jokes come to mind." She chewed on her lips. "Jokes are flotation devices on the great sea of sorrowful life. They are the exit signs in a very dark room."

"But you're a sight gag person." He stalled. "I remember you zigging and zagging on that unicycle."

"Yes. Eventually there were insurance issues."

"What did you end up doing with it?"

"The uni?"

"Yeah."

"Sold it on eBay."

"That's right. You had a whole eBay thing going there for a while."

The litter box still slid around in the backseat.

"Remember, before Crater, our cats Lumpling and Dumpling?"

"Sure," he said.

"And how when Dumpling had to be put down Lumpling didn't understand? There was the vet on a house call in the basement administering the lethal injection, and there was Lumpling prancing around saying, Hello, hello, happy to see everybody! Even when Dumpling was dead. And then Dumpling was taken away and Lumpling didn't understand and fell into great despondency over the months, searching the house for Dumpling, day after day, until a thorny malignant growth burst through into his sinuses and he too began to die."

"So I'm Lumpling," Finn said.

There was a silence longer than most of their silences. Finally she said, "You'd rather be Dumpling?"

"Why do you want to be Dumpling? You don't have to be Dumpling if you don't want to."

She nodded. "I'll think about it."

He nodded too. "It's a hard time for men and women. It's a hard time for us."

"Men and women. Yeah. You know, one of the things I always liked about you? You were not one of those men-and-women men. You were never one of those questionable guys who said, 'I really like women.'"

Finn was quiet for a moment. "But I do like women."

"Ach! Now you've gone and ruined it."

Though they were moving forward down the moody road, the road seemed instead to be rushing toward them, so that they were like needles being threaded. On either side of the speeding asphalt the grasses were yellow, twisted, and flat. And on his side the broken center line blitzed by like a ticker tape.

"Remember that time you helped me make a Lincoln's birthday cake for my students, and we sifted all that flour, and the kitchen looked like it had snowed inside?"

"It's always snowing inside," she said, gnomic and perhaps distracted.

"What is sifting for anyway?"

"To find the gold. To find the prize."

"That's right. To find the prize and grate it to death. You were good at that."

"Thanks."

"Which necropolis are we headed to again?" he asked. It was as if they both kept putting it out of their minds.

"The Blue Deaths Can Sometimes Matter one. The forensic moonshiners. The dead all laid out above ground like a battle-field still in battle."

"That's right. Jesus."

"All remains to be seen. Get it?"

"You want to drive?"

She closed her eyes. "You didn't want this trip? You didn't want me to make an appearance back there in the green cemetery and present myself to you?"

"I didn't know you just needed a ride."

"I didn't *just* need a ride."

Finn's throat began to close.

"I also wanted to see you, Finn," she said. "That was certainly part of it. To know you were all right."

"Part of it? Well, I'm obviously not all right."

"You're going to need my motivation here to be totally about you?" she asked. "You want the whole mournful play to yourself?"

"Yeah. I wanted the whole fucking mournful play to myself. Jesus, Lily: you are pitiless."

The wind that broke from her was not the usual wind of death. It contained the rustle of leaves and a kind of back-to-school song and the old sachet of thawed frozen dinner.

"You think because of my—condition—I don't have feelings?" she asked.

He scratched his head. "What do the people do again at this
place we're going to?"

"They study your body to find out who the murderer is and
how long he has been on the lam. Most murderers are on the
lam for a while. I'm helping to solve crimes."

"Whatever happened to your desire to be a crash test
dummy? Automotive safety seems a noble cause."

"That's in Motor City. The other direction. Yes, a test-crash
cadaver. I'm not a good driver."

"You don't have to be the driver. The dummy doesn't drive.
At least not always. I'm driving. I can turn around right now."

"Oh, yeah. See? I'm so dumb. It's like I've already been in a
crash. It's as if I've already slammed my head into the rearview
mirror. It's as if I've already hurtled my chest into the glove compartment and split my heart in two like an apple."

Spare me, Finn did not say. Nor *Always with the apples.* "I
suppose at this police site they do things like test the mineral
level of the fetching twinkle in your eye. The number and nature
of the beetles swarming over your personal gelatin."

"They do indeed do things like that."

"Perhaps we should go back to singing. We could sing Beatles songs for a kind of entomological theme."

"Don't you love farce?"

"That's not a Beatles song."

"My fault . . . I thought that you'd want what I want."

"No," Finn said.

"Aren't we a pair? Me here at last in—or, on—the ground."

"I never liked that song."

"Nobody likes that song. Still, it was our theme song at the clown office. You gotta love your theme song. Be true to your school."

"I never worked anywhere that had a theme song."

"Well, let me tell you, you really missed out."

"Do you know anything by Death Cab for Cutie?"

"Uh, no," she said. "I don't."

He was quiet for a moment. "Don't you want people gathered around paying you tribute by singing songs?"

She exhaled a kind of snotty snort. "Uh, you're joking, right."

He slowed then stopped to avoid two turkeys with silver heads and sable feathers, crossing casually as if they'd never seen a car on this road before.

"Don't you want something real? A headstone? A marker of any sort? So I can come visit?"

While they were waiting for the turkeys to be done with their gobble and bobble, he looked over at her. She had gone into her hundred-yard stare out the windshield. There was a fading to her skin, the way a bee dead on a winter windowsill had no more yellow. She seemed to be chewing gum but it was surely just the inside of her cheek. "Do *you* want that? a headstone?" she asked absently. The odor of pond scum wafted off her teeth when she spoke.

He now decided the sky was a better place for looking and he leaned over the dashboard to look up and through the windshield. Could Venus rise in the afternoon? Or was that Jupiter? And why was the human race so interested in Mars and not Venus? Venus was close. It was love. It was the murky past. But all the clues to the future were there, though located where they always were: in the past. So time travel. Someday it would be managed.

He leaned back against his seat. "Me? For myself? I want a nice medium-sized rock that glitters a little on a sunny day. I want it to be near a picnic table. And I want it engraved with my name, address, and phone number."

"Your phone number." She moved her jaw around, again as if she were chewing gum. "Don't you want a little maudlin quote that sums up your life?"

"Yeah. I want *WELL, THAT WAS WEIRD.*"

"All caps."

Actually, he wanted only the conventional thing. A stone tablet covered in lichen in the churchyard by the church on Church Street. "All caps. Also, *GOT NO EMOJIS FOR THIS.*"

"Also, *ATTENTION: UNDERLYING CONDITIONS.*"

The turkeys had finally crossed and he started up again.

The pathetic trees and dead underbrush zipped by, and to take his mind off Lily for a moment he concentrated on gene splicing, George Harrison, leaf-cutter bees, and of course the fiery, blinking pinpricks of the planets. He resumed his contemplation of what seemed to him a puzzle. Why did everyone want to travel to Mars again? Would they like a Martian destination wedding? One should want simply to prevent a Venutian fate.

He could not believe where he was driving.

The moon no longer seemed to be rising but to be in a lunar standstill. A gibbous waxed almost to the point of full.

He could not believe where he was taking her.

A meteor hovered low on the horizon without movement then blitzed away. It was almost evening again. He and Lily would once again be driving at night. The staring stars and their magnificent rudeness would not deter the two of them. The dippers, the gods, the warriors all flickering about the ambiguous emoji of the moon. Finn's own particular universe and its nothingness was down here.

"Did you enjoy Jack?"

"What?"

"You heard me."

"Eh?" she said, her running deafness joke. Then she added, "I was pretending with Jack. The whole thing with him was pretend."

"How about with me?" He was changing his mind about everything. The wheeling ceiling of the stars: Who were the two of them with their trivial wretchedness beneath the icy fire overhead?

"Yeah. No," she said. "With you? I was pretending a lot less." She looked out the window. "Love cannot occur unless you are free to love. You have to be free or it's not love."

Here he knew she was speaking of her illness. Of the extra room of the mind that was the suicide room and lit up and flung its doors open. Of the bruising bash against the killing glass. But he leapt in anyway. "No! Love is a feeling and condition that seldom waits for perfect circumstances. One can love in a hospital or a prison or in a war."

"No, one can't. Not really."

"One can love one's captor."

"That is Stockholm syndrome," said Lily.

"The Swedes know a lot about love."

"Yeah. The land of the midnight sun. You can paint your house all night there if you want."

"Have you become the unquiet dead? A garrulous ghost?"

"I guess. I suppose at this late stage in the game I could be quieter."

He just kept driving. "Don't be quieter," he said.

Lily went again into her hundred-yard gaze. Where was the wide receiver? Oh, right: here.

"I was the she-wolf in the Arctic documentary," she finally said. "Searching for a place to have her hypothetical pups. I never found it. It was so damn cold and the snow came and went then came again. That's when howling began and strange male wolves approached."

"And one of them was me."

"And one of them was not."

Out the window the bedheads of the keening, windblown trees waved their branches in screeching, stretching yawns.

"Remember when we visited the moon and people watched us on TV?" she asked.

"I do."

"That was fun."

"We got right in there into the moon's grin."

"More a grimace."

"The moon's winking grimace. And then we built a fire on the dark side of the moon to signal that we were there and fine and ready to leave. We memorized the swiftly retreating galaxies, feeling more alone than ever in the universe."

"Remember when I found you in that smashed-up space-ship in New Mexico and had to take you home?"

"Had to."

"Everything's worth doing at least once. I suppose."

"Maybe we're just not all that bright."

She sighed. "We'll never know."

Dearest Sister:
          The sheriff seems not to care. Or not to believe Ofelia. Not certain which. Or something else entirely. Though I expect the law to come knocking soon it hasn't yet. It has occurred to me that Ofelia, who busies herself downstairs as I write, might have grown frightened and not told the sheriff anything at all. She might have simply walked around the block. So now I am in a pickle. A pickle is a thing I understand. Plus I am now indeed all the Elizabethan things Jack once uttered in the show business of his own mind—the faithless wench, the wretched bitch-wolf, the fusty nut with no kernel—which despite my name and hospitality I cannot accommodate with much comprehension at all. I had once heard him say each of these things about other people.

          Instead I asked Ofelia if we had enough cornmeal for the week.

          "I believe so, Miss Libby. I also ordered some more butter and tea at the store. Miss Ann has charged it to your account."

          "More tea," I said as if it were a mysterious item I was just getting accustomed to.

"Just a pound," she added. "Ceylonese."

"Well that's excellent," I said then hurried away.

I need the preacher to stop by here and conversate a little. I need him to say daft and holy things and fix his face into a compassionate mask. He will be tedious and lulling and the rhythm of my breaths will be returned to steadiness. He will seek to brighten and disperse the shadows in my heart and his attempts will amuse me and summon admiration though not much else. I have no confession plans. Still, I remain vainly interested in heaven.

Yours down here still.
Eliz.

"What are we doing again?"

"What do you mean?"

"Are we flying?" murmured Lily. They had just sailed over a little hill in the road. "I'm getting a Chitty Chitty Bang Bang feeling. I would like to feel we are cheerful as larks, singing mid-air. But I don't know." She looked down at her own abdomen. "It's like I've grown a seat pocket with water landing instructions. *Entrails* is not a good word, is it?"

"You are visceral. Full of fateful auguries."

"My body a gauzy purse."

Finn could feel the ticking of her life against the windows of the car. The papery edges of her had fallen in on themselves, and she had gone from origami to a wad.

"Y'OK?" he asked.

"I'm feeling at moments like I'm not on the highway but trudging along on the frontage road."

While keeping his eyes on the driving, he moved his head briefly against her. "I can feel the muffled pumping of your heart."

"The muffled pumpkin?"

"Pumping."

"I wonder if we got all the mud out of my ears. Y'know? Here's another thing: I realize it's coming up, but Halloween is very insulting to the dead. I'm just starting to understand that. It's insensitive and incorrect. Why do people insult the dead with all the splayed skeletons and ghosts and stuffed 'people' with rubber knives in their chests. The dead are trying to love us! To invite us! This is the tacky thanks they get."

"Invite?"

Perhaps he and Lily had moved out of controlled hallucination into random reality shards. Finn eased off the gas. Between them, in the car, was the electric atmosphere of a clash of wills. He no longer felt like himself. But also no longer felt like some attribute of her. He felt the light jangle of discord, the condition and feeling of every home he'd ever entered. To their left and right were low undulating walls of rough fieldstone.

"I guess we're getting closer," Finn said.

"That's sweet of you to say," she murmured.

"No, I mean to the place."

When the voice of the car's GPS came on it directed them down a long county pike and then down a dirt lane indicated by a DEAD END sign, at which point Finn knew they had almost arrived.

"Dead end," read Lily.

The rutted road to the body farm was lined with leggy hackberry trees. The tires threw stones up into the metal quarter panels of the car. The riverbed bottom of the lane had gentle ridges like the roof of a mouth.

There was a second small sign: FORENSIC AREA. NO TRESPASSING.

Forgive us our trespasses.

"People are always led into temptation. And they follow. One wrestles with it with conviction but not much power. Oh, well," said Lily. "I'm in overtime at this point, but I need to google the rules."

"I think in the postseason playoffs it's sudden death."

"Well, I kind of mucked up the sudden part."

"The coin toss matters. Possession matters."

"Possession," she said. She pretended to mull this over. "What are we actually talking about here?"

"What are we ever talking about." He cut the engine and all was still. He kept the keys in the ignition and let the headlights shine.

The body farm itself seemed to be behind and adjacent to an actual farm, as if the body field had filled with farmers who had just given up, wandered over, and laid themselves down to die. He could ask her to save him a seat in heaven but she would just shake her head and say, "What makes you think I got invited to *that* party," or some such thing, and the shaking of her head would cause it to twist at an odd unfixable angle until she resembled a gooseneck lamp with a broken shade.

The headlight on Lily's side suddenly went out and the car was left with only one beam shining into the waist-high dung-hued grass like a flashlight. In lieu of a flashlight.

"How do we get over this fence?" asked Lily.

Finn could see a sagging part of the fence that anyone could step over. But he didn't point it out. "We wait for the deepest part of night." He could feel a kind of fury taking over him.

"Oh, Mr. Gloaming Gloom." She turned and fixed him with a stare of bewildering sparkle. "Always with the dark. Believe me. It's not as if I don't understand."

"I want you in the world, where you belong," he suddenly said.

"Perhaps the world where I belong is exactly where I'm going."

"Your spacecraft hovers? Your mother ship awaits?" He tapped his fingers then slammed his hand against the steering wheel.

"Baby, you've lost that lovin' feeling," she said.

"I'm sad that you're leaving. And that you didn't have a good time." He tried not to cry. "I'm sorry I'm not reason enough for you to try." He knew the illness didn't work that way. One was not supposed to take it personally. But fuck that.

"I had a good time or two. Besides, Finn, it's not your responsibility. You're not the host."

"I am the host! I am at least the host of my own life!"

"You're not the caterer. And you don't own the restaurant."

He was getting lost. "I need some takeout!"

"What?"

"Damn it, Lily!"

"You drove me here, Finn. I mean, you were driving."

"These GPSs are nuts! The car seemed to have its own wild logic," he pleaded. "I've changed my mind. It's not too late for you to change yours. I know you can do it."

"Oh, Finn. I'm just a bump in your road. Perhaps like the one we just went over it will give you a little liftoff feeling."

"No—it looks like I'm just a bump in yours."

"You are a beautiful person with years ahead of you. Forget about me." She seemed to be trying to smile sympathetically. The circles beneath her eyes had gone a briny green. Her eyelids too. There was just mournful silence now between them. "I don't expect you to understand us depleted people who only see the exit sign and want to head there. It's just who we are. Not really a choice. Just as your not understanding probably isn't a choice. But thank you for taking me along the scenic route."

"Yes, this tweaky hellscape was epically immersive. But I didn't see you buy any postcards in the shop."

"Oops. Yes, postcards. Now you're taking me to the dark place."

"That's a laugh."

"See? There you go. Was that so hard?" A piece of pain seemed to be traveling up from her gut and making its way across her face to escape.

"Lily, don't you see that"—and now he could hear the absurdity of his own words as they were forming, flapping, flying—"that we belong together? I know you have never been able to find a through-line through the indifference of the universe . . . but I can be a stay against that. I am not part of the indifference."

Her expression of mirth was so dry it was like seven kinds of grit in his face. "Oh, my god, Finn. All your despair and insistence—what is it for?"

He shifted uneasily, switching his tack. It was her condition that mangled all the hope. Also killed the illusions that contained the hope, like soap bubbles that contained rainbowed air before they burst. She was wedded to eventual obliteration on every front. If she couldn't win she would work hard to fail. The in-between places where real life occurred weren't detectable on her radar. That too was the illness: the faulty radar. "When I say together," he said, "I mean, together living on the same hellish planet at the same hellish time. I don't need you to love me. I'm not sure I ever needed that. I have my own love for you. I have my brother. I have my job. I just need your willingness to try."

She looked around. "This place could use some patio furniture."

"I want you to marry me," he said.

"You are proposing to me?"

"I guess. Yes. I am."

His grievesome girl, his brackish belle, his Diamond Lil: Yes, say yes.

He had never asked for much but now her laugh was an unambiguous blast: "Ha!"

He believed the arc and position of her mouth constituted a true smile. Maybe. He fashioned a smile in return.

Because it was now or never for the smiles, for the request, for everything. In fact, before now it had been never, but he wanted to fix that, to make time move backward, to make the air grow warmer and lighter, to fire the continuity staff of Mother Nature and God. "There's gotta be a judge, a clerk, a partner, a witness somewhere nearby. Can I get a witness. Look!" He pulled a bar of soap from the tourist lodge out of his pocket. "A Cashmere Bouquet to throw at one of the bridesmaids. Doesn't matter if the clerk is also the bridesmaid. I meant to ask before, Lily. I always meant to ask. Now I'm begging, which, let's face it, has gone out of style. People don't beg much nowadays."

"No, they don't."

"But I am. I'm begging." It was all hopeless: like Eurydice, she'd grown fonder of the underworld. Hijacked by death. Beggars couldn't also be choosers.

Or perhaps she was not Eurydice but just some irrelevant lovely bug, something with the skitter of a beetle, the group-kamikaze of an ant, the horned ass of an earwig. Human pleas were useless. He felt a little desperate and overwhelmed. She was a hauntologist: a destroyer of futures, dangerous and ridiculous. Yet one always had to hold on to someone like her. One had to challenge oneself and also, let's face it, protect society. Because what was love about if not that. Protecting society from all the crazy things you knew your beloved was. Of course perhaps he had gotten some scrambled memos and read from them randomly or skimmed them all with only one tired eye.

"Won't they realize you haven't done the proper paperwork?" he said. " 'Here's a corpse with no paperwork! Who's ever heard of such a thing?' "

"You are something. Also you have a lot of rules all of a sudden."

"Yeah?" Why had he just said *yeah* so hopefully? "I still love you, Lily."

"Don't make me snap my fingers all around your head," she warned.

She was getting out of the car, pressing on the side of it for balance. She then opened the back door on the passenger's side, shoved the litter box over, and sat down to put on her clown shoes, which earlier she had taken off. "I always feel a little in disguise when I'm not wearing these." He and Lily had perhaps now reached a part of the play where the costumes mattered. Finn was wearing his WE WERE TOGETHER—FORGET THE REST T-shirt, but he was wearing a thick sweater over it. He too got out of the car to walk around and stand next to her in the night while she put on her shoes. There was no stopping her, he guessed. And of course, as she had pointed out, he was the one who had driven her here.

The cold was both bitter and soft and there was some snow—why was it snowing in the South?—leisurely, theatrical snow, which used to seem picturesque but now filled him with dread, once more like the third act of *La Bohème*. There was never going to be a proper fourth, or rather the acts now would sort of fuse, just repeating in a different opera altogether: *No More Rice Krispies,* over and over.

"I will miss your rogue and random energy!" he cried.

She stared at him with a checked-out expression that then stirred and focused. "I will miss—your dogged cluelessness." Her smile was a wan smudge. Her teeth chartreuse. Her hands and neck a darkening cellophane. He could see now she was starting again to have the face of a drowned person, the wide eyes, the seaweed tresses.

"I mean that with love," she added. The snow was steady and silencing. It stuck in both their hair, scarcely melting, like confetti. There was no music. He tried not to imagine that each flake was one of his own tears evaporated from the ground then in a cold cloud remade scornfully to drop back down and jeer.

"This really isn't ending like a Broadway musical," he said.

"No. Never liked them the way you did."

"But the clown song—that's from a musical."

"Again, Finn: that was a song we sang at work. As a joke. It was a jokey work song."

Her work was a pseudocult of theatrical entrepreneurs, a cross between *Rosemary's Baby* and the March of Dimes. A vocation. An avocation. A havocation. She opened her palm and revealed a red plastic nose. "Look what I found. Someone apparently put it in my shoe. To prevent blisters maybe." It was crushed a bit but she still put it on her nose. "The other cadavers are gonna love this." She looked at him wistfully it seemed. "Tell people I was fun."

"You weren't that fun."

"Aw, have a heart."

"I'm not buying your bullshit, Lily. The way you have allowed all the bad weather in your head to shower itself on—" He hadn't meant to say *shower*. "You have to refuse death. Resist it—"

"I'm going to need you to wrap up this little lecture of yours." Lily got up with her shoes loosely tied and snapped her fingers all around his head. The energy of it surprised him. "Now come in close and give me a kiss goodbye."

He said nothing. He was still recovering from the finger-snapping. Her body now seemed vestigial, the lingering registration of an idea—like a man's nipples.

"Yeah, well, OK then, you'll know where to find me," she said. Her head nodded sort of up at the sky and sort of down toward the possessive ground and also vaguely to her right. It was a nod that said, *Yonder.* She began to walk. "I guess this is what you'd call twilight," she said, "though I have no idea what time it is."

He believed it was getting closer to dawn.

He decided to follow, but she was outpacing him. "You can't get off the hook this easily," he called after her. "You can't not see your life through! Of course there's suffering and it's all hard! Of course God is such a withholding bigshot he didn't bother to show us every last page of the existence contract." Finn didn't know if this was better than "I cannot live without you and will no longer try!" which he also called out.

It almost stopped her. She did pause for a moment. "You will no longer try? Wow, you really seem to have changed your mind."

"I didn't really understand our destination."

"You didn't understand our destination?" she repeated with some mockery. "You were driving."

Once more with the driving. The endless yellow signs and the stalled-out road construction and the infinitude of trucks. "No, I didn't understand! Not in an actual way!"

"Are you suggesting that I haven't really thought this through? Or that *you* haven't? Are you implying that I don't own my own death?"

"*Own* it? As in you have a deed?"

"Sure. I have a deed." She now strangely seemed able to walk rather fast. "I'm headed for the natural habitat of my species!" she called back.

"Yes!" he shouted. "Time to get back to your bonnie lair!"

It was hard for him to keep up. Maybe this was how it always had been when they went for walks. Some suppressed memories were now coming back to him.

But it did not keep him from calling out, "Everything is about you and your sorrow! Everything is attended to at your convenience! You're going to bury yourself—look!—beneath a full moon with its Buster Keaton face. Or, practically a full moon. The sky's gotten decked out for you." The sky had shed its filmy haze and seemed instead full of geysers, as if painted by Van Gogh. Self-pity—repellent and laced with wrath—stewed in him. "Why, Lily? Why at this time? Why did you do all this? Everything! You knew my brother—my brother was dying!—" And here he started to choke, for he could feel now that his brother was dying right then at that very moment, just as he uttered these words; in his mind's eye he saw his brother's gaze fasten on him sharply but with kindness, then vanish. He could hear the last pounding of Max's heart on the hard door of time. The World Series must have concluded. He now no longer had his brother even though just a minute ago he had insisted he did.

Lily again turned to Finn—was that an expression of compassion or pity? She suddenly came half-floating half-flying back toward him, her mouth a gash, her hair a storm, her skin a putrid pewter. She held his face gingerly in her trowel-like hands. "Look at me," she said to him. "Life is very little. It's kind of a canary coop. A speck in the air."

"It's my current address," he replied hotly. His eyes began to well. "What will I do with all that chicken-fried fried—"

"What?"

"—chicken?"

She sighed. "Don't you see, Finn? You aren't really seeing. We are surrounded by death so that we can be taught to accept it."

"Homeopathy?"

"Maybe," she said.

"But your whole vocation, your clown thing, was supposed to be a distraction from death! That was your job."

"I guess I just sucked at it." She shut her eyes for a moment. "But you knew that."

"Well, here's something else that I need to know." He could tell he was wearing his jilted-at-the-altar face. She was wearing a look that said, *Even in death I have to report in to your desire?*

"What?" Her teeth were like little nuts.

"Is the afterlife expensive? I mean, do you get to the other side and discover nothing is free? That they charge you for everything?"

"For fuck's sake," she murmured.

"Sorry. I've been a little worried about my finances."

"Listen to me," she said with some tenderness. "Everything is going to be OK." In her personal revolutions she was like an unrotating planet with a permanent dark side and a permanent light side where the sun never set. She had always been like that. Was there a line in between, a sweet Goldilocks zone? No, in this tale Goldilocks was devoured by the bears and the zone was just a permanently positional stripe of rising hope, which was also a stripe of permanently positional sinking hope.

"You're just going to leave me here?" he asked.

"You want gas money?" She raised her eyebrows and let go, stepped back, an opalescent figure and face. Above the clown nose her eyes blackened and emptied, losing their interested gaze in exchange for bleak determination.

"I'm jealous of the damn dirt," he said. "I realize it's over— but I can't let go," he added.

"Isn't that, like, a song?"

"Oh, I'm sure it is very much like a song."

"One does not die all at once. There are stages."

"I've gathered. And one does not grieve all at once. But there really aren't stages, as advertised. There's just a kind of sad soup of the day."

"I'm grateful for your driving. And for so many other things."

"Words." He tried to make his face contemptuously still, but he suspected affection showed regardless.

"Well. I've assembled them and give them to you."

"I'm afraid of your desertion. Your self-desertion. Your desertion of everything." Punishing scorn was hard for him to summon or depict. He understood now that she had had to return to him, to make her reappearance to him, because he was the only person who would have actually believed it was her.

Turning, she seemed to recede, her figure narrow, flowing, moving briskly again, toward the several areas of broken-down fence. Her mental light had begun that day like a strobe, wild and disorganized, but now was focused and on track.

One final time she spun slowly, to add, with her red nose still on and her finger in the air, "Gonna rap on your door."

"What? You have the meaning of that song backward!" he called exegetically out to her. Instead of music and sadness and loss, he now felt an unfinished argument in the air. "He was my only brother, Lily! You have smashed my life to bits! Look! Everything is at your convenience! You're going to bury yourself of course—that is unfortunate. But the sky has helpfully arranged the full moon and other fancy lights for you to do it by!" He was repeating himself. And maybe fibbing a little: the moon was not quite full. It seemed to be waning already. A sliver gone from the gold.

She then yelled hoarsely into the night: "Finn! For God's sake! Don't be a dick!"

Her shout was woeful but matter-of-fact and like the woodwinds of the Venetian-masked swans her voice had a fading reverb. It reminded him of the Pink Floyd records of his youth, records that had really belonged to Max and that used to break his heart when in the afternoons after school he had lain there listening to them without his brother's permission. Finn had grown up with a nut allergy, a speech impediment, a crush on a sewing dummy. Inevitably, his life would have had to include this crazy scene. How could it not. Of course the nut allergy managed to be intermittent. The sewing dummy clearly not so much.

Lily's red shoes shone in the brush. Even her nose caught a

little moonlight. The rest of her was a swirl of white paper in a windy vacant field.

He had followed her, over the fallen wire fence on into the night, but now stopped. She was climbing over yet another fence. Some of her paper robe stuck to some wire but she tugged at it enough for it to rip free. She became a receding cocoon.

He turned back toward the car. The dull live ache of day-to-day had entered him. He stepped back over the bent wire. He was done. What was the point of anything. There had been so much he had clung to, so much he had needed her to do through the years which she just couldn't do. Now he didn't need anything. Death had flirted with her mind then taken her entire being on a never-ending adventure-date, and that was that.

There were occasions, of course, when it was not inappropri-ate to want to shoot oneself. Short of that, there was always the go-to eye-stabbing.

"You are dead to me!" he called over his shoulder, with only a slight turn of his head.

If he had more fully turned his head, he would have seen her, in full bioluminescence, shining from her own uncajolable deadness, lying down on the ground, slipping beneath the soil and disappearing on a hillside near a toolshed. If he had turned his head. Yet he would not turn his head. He would not. But then he did. And saw nothing.

S ister mine:
　　My fate today is full of clover. I had been fretting over what to do about monsieur. But fortune smiled, and like a magic trick a lawyer man named Mister Phinneus Bates paid a visit with a pony-drawn wagon. He handed me an embossed calling card and said he had heard I had a certain lodger in the house and that said lodger had died and the body was not yet claimed.

It was as if this Mr. Phinneus thought he were Joseph of Arimathea. Which since no one knows where Arimathea is, and the scripture doesn't indicate, might be Chattanooga.

"Well, sir, I have to ask where you might have heard that?" In a tavern, I assumed. Though not one in Turkeytail. "From the sheriff?"

"Sheriffs have deputies and word travels fast, ma'am," he said. "Out and about there are some persons who believe they know who this dead man of yours might be."

Perhaps Jack the boarder had seeded his own rumors. I did not know whether he had the right eye color for who they all thought he was, but that would be no problem if I could stick the eyes shut with goat glue.

"What will you do with him? The federals are doing experiments on dead bodies since the war," I said. "Is that what you want him for? Cadaver practice to see his stopping power in the back of the head while watching a play?"

"No, ma'am."

And that's when I knew he was just going to cart Jack around from county fair to magic show to carnival to roadside circus. "Well, I am something of a sawed-in-half lady myself," I said. I could see now Jack was going to be spending eternity with the midget lady and the bearded lady and the four-legged lady. Would that be enough ladies for him? "He's all yours. I could use his room. I will give him to you for rent owed."

"Well, ma'am, that might be a deal."

I told him that as they did in days of old I had covered the body in honey and tansy oil, then poured bourbon over the top. It was preserving. I left out that I resisted the temptation of lighting a match. He said that in the wagon he had a chair, a table, some candles stashed inside. Also a small apothecary in a large leather bag.

"In case you get the quincy or the farcy?" I asked. Remember we said that all the time as children? I tried to give him a little smile.

He just nodded. He had not doffed his hat which is the primary reason I do not refer to him as a gentleman. Also? He wanted to trundle Jack from fair ground to fair ground. Well, it was cleaner for the earth and any vegetables that might grow in it, I suppose, to just wheel him around like that.

"One thing," I added. "I don't want anyone coming round claiming rights to any ostensible pensions. He claimed to have both a Union one and a Confederate one. Though I seldom hear of a Confederate one anywhere though he boasted to possess one, putting all the payments deposited in a Montreal bank,

I believe. Money traveled a little slowly for him. At least it seemed to."

"Send anyone my way. I'm an attorney and I can take care of his business affairs. Address is on the card."

"Well. Good." I stuck the card in my belt. "I think we will all feel gay when Johnny comes marching home," I said, to sudden silence on his part. "But I wonder if you might come back end of the day, today or tomorrow, after sunset, and then we can get this matter done with."

"Yes, ma'am." He touched his hat.

Then I added, "Just don't present him as a Christian. He wasn't that."

And so, dear sister, Mr. Phinneus Bates came that very night and I traded him the body for rent owed. He went upstairs with me where Ofelia and I had wrapped the handsome now dead boarder in a sheet, trying not to look too hard at the stub of mutton that was his lost leg, and then had rolled him into an oval rug, an item I was sad to lose. I had thrown his cork-and-wood prosthetic with the leather straps into the rolling for good measure. Priscilla briefly emerged from her room, desperately wondering about the meal schedule the next day, but I shooed her away with a grimace. It had to be done. "There's noodles and greens aplenty which I'll be fixing. No cause for you to be worrying," I chided her. I couldn't have bungle after bungle.

"Oh, I'm terribly sorry, Miss Libby," she said and closed her door until morning.

Thus Mr. Phinneus and I carried him down the stairs together. I could feel the hard fake leg on my side. I had glued shut Mr. Jack's now (in all ways) unsightly eyes, but Mr. Phinneus didn't care to maneuver aside the rug and shine a light to study the face for confirmation. He had a traveling show in mind and the face could be tinkered with, I supposed, to conform to what a killer looked like. Not that anyone ever really knew. It was God's constant surprise.

Or perhaps Mr. Phinneus just wanted to ride around with the body. But first he would take him straight away to an embalmer that could do mummies. Or he suggested as much. He stood by the wagon, wiping his hands on his trousers.

"He's got a whole trunk of tights. Don't you want his trunk of tights?" I asked.

"No, ma'am I certainly do not," he replied.

"There's some doublets and fine looking swords still in their scabbards."

By next week I would slice all the tights up with the swords and begin braiding them into a rug much like the one I was losing.

"No, thank you."

I could see in the wagon he had a metal Fisk and Raymond casket. Looked like that in the evening air.

"A true sarcophagus," I said, nodding in that direction.

"It's very preserving," he said, a word we both had on our minds, and then I knew for certain he would make a mummy from Mr. Jack and take him on a tour. He would move him into the casket down the line when he had more manpower.

"I will respect his remains," he said.

"I certainly don't much care." And then a coughing fit took hold. And when I came back to myself, I added, "Or rather: good. Do your best."

"After they shot up that redhead in the tobacco barn years back, word was he had made it all the way to India. But I felt sure he was in these parts. Like Jesse James."

"Jesse James," I scoffed but recovered my tone, because I

suddenly remembered Mr. James as a boarder here once, two years back, though he neglected to sign the guestbook. "Well yes. One is always hearing flashy and terrifying news."

At moments like these I often feel the growing romantic curtain being lowered over the war. The many vibrating worlds in front and behind, within and without, intersecting and yet not intersecting.

"I've got a pair of Kit Carson's moccasins and one of his boots," he added. "Also Stonewall Jackson's arm."

"That so," I said, though I feared it sounded like "fatso."

He covered up the back wagon seat with a tarp then turned toward me and finally doffed his hat for a split minute. The bridled pony up front was bobbing his head. He was about to begin a long whirligig road trip with a corpse, something of a tradition in these parts, I'm afraid. Part puppet show, part medicine tent, part parade. Plus the celebrity footwear and stray appendage. Perhaps some slushy ice on a waffle. I predict a sad ending in a hobo camp.

"Thank you kindly, ma'am." He took some money out of a horse-scrotum purse to pay me. "I am obliged."

I just looked at him. "Don't thank me. It's business," I said, taking the money, and he nodded and put his hat back on then headed in the same direction as the miners and the fancy girls, the bushwhackers and the sow.

I went back in to find Ofelia. "Well, Miss Ofelia, I reckon that was that," I said.

"That was that, all right," she said, shaking her head and wiping her hands on her green gingham apron. Her daresomeness was returning. Her posture straightened, so I straightened mine as well. She shook her head as if to get hair out of her eyes and events out of her thoughts. We never spoke of these matters again.

The pastor will visit next week, I believe, and it will be good for me to see an unvexed person. I look forward to the parlor trick of his intermittent consolation. My secret to living right now—to go to bed every night with two things to do the next day that serve the world—needs an adjustment. I need to be adjacent to some divinity, to catch it a little without its being warranted.

I often wonder whatever was that long ago hatred that sprang up briefly between you and me? It seemed an accident that would not go away. It was a shamelessness that was countered with envy and judgment. It produced shrinkage and dislocation, and soon we had turned our ankles and then our eyes. Was it the war? One would like to say no matter, but the matter finds new ways to continue, like a snaking river.

If I could sing you'd be the song. But I was never good at singing. And there aren't many songs that I know. Of course there are the church ones. Honey, I do like Jesus. I just don't like a single song about him. Nor his mean, lying crystal ball when he said, "The poor will always be with us" because there are many poor people that have completely disappeared.

You are in my thoughts every hour. On a windless night I hear your voice—lord I do.

> Your loving
> Eliz.

Ps: I used your ashes this past January outside on the icy stairs for the safe walking of the boarders. I felt strongly you wouldn't mind being put to good use.

In Finn's NoMad hotel room the minibar hummed and burned blue like the electric ice cube of God. Below in the street small groups were marching. It was two days after Election Day and a group in the street below was marching and chanting, "Please reject our President." A half hour later what appeared to be another group marched down the opposite way, chanting and holding signs saying, PLEASE RESPECT OUR PRESIDENT. They could almost be the same groups, but from his view on the ninth floor he could see that there were differences: the group rejecting was younger by and large. And the group respecting had a lot of people painted in red, white, and blue and a big maize-haired boy was pushing a wheelchair in which was slumped a mummified-looking dark-haired man, wearing an old black frock coat and vest, a string tie and midthigh leather boots, though he was of course sitting and looked more like he'd been thrown from a horse and just landed there than like he had any plans for riding one. A red wool blanket had been spread diagonally across his lap; atop it was a pistol with the curve of a derringer, which he patted like a pet.

This time Finn had flown to New York, so he did not have

his car. His electric toothbrush had accidentally switched on and vibrated in his carry-on bag the entire time—he had thought it was something wrong with the plane. When he traveled he sometimes suspended his project of testing his sanity by seeing if *The New York Times* would print his online responses. He had other ways to guess how he was doing. Like just guessing.

Yesterday he had found Max's crematorium and gone there, watching someone else burn because even for this he had arrived too late for Max. And so he honored a homeless man in a body bag whose only relatives were two nieces in Maine. No one was present to bear witness so Finn volunteered. The city official allowed it. After the quick rasp of the unzipping of the bag, they pulled the man straight into the incinerator. Finn stood between the official and the crematorium director, ten feet from the furnace and said "Amen" over and over, hearing the snap of the heated body when it sprang up, then tipped and burst. The director filmed the first half hour on his cellphone though he was just filming a closed hot door.

Now today was Max's service. Was it St. Barnabas or St. Gabriel or St. Dominic? He had the Bronx address he needed to find the little church where his brother's funeral was. The service was at eleven. Midmorning he went downstairs and hailed a cab. The parades had avoided rush hour, mostly, and traffic was light, though the groups chanting would suddenly emerge like trick-or-treaters in a sidewalk then pass. He had never understood this city though he had lived here once. Now the tallest buildings he had ever seen blocked the beautiful Roman light that used to also grace New York. "Take FDR, yes?" he said. For if he could get on the East Side, near water, in the morning, the world might briefly seem resilient and oblivious to all the human drama that was killing it. And as Finn watched the river's opaque and stubborn strength he would try not to think too much about how long Max had held on, how it seemed, the hospice people had said to him, as if Max were waiting for someone.

The priest knew that his brother and his brother's family weren't Catholic, but Max's wife had arranged for this, and this was what pastors and priests were for: the gentle handling of families going through unfathomable things. The big adieu. Finn was grateful for the professional know-how. Grateful for a gentle, smiling Dominican priest who knew English and could lead them through this swamp of hours. The pews were oak and bare. Finn did not kneel on the bench. He would try not to zone out during the readings and hymns, but his attention came and went. The service seemed to bear no resemblance to the story of his brother's life. He supposed these things were spiritual gestures for the self and to the extent it kept widows and children company, who was anyone to judge this moral puppet show? Did anyone really know what the story of a human life ever was? There were so many competing and intersecting and sometimes parallel and obliterating narratives. He sat there as remarks about life and death swirled around him. In life's wrestle with death there was much suffering, and in death a diabolical vanishing. Suffering then vanishing. Suffering then vanishing. Did everyone understand that's what they had signed up for, or really just not signed up at all but been drafted? Life was soldiering. Death was disappearance. Death sure had the power move. It had the black cape, the fine print, and the magic tricks. Life was stuck with sundries from the corner PX.

Scripture continued to be read nonsensically. There were more psalms set to music. Some idea of Max himself was in the eye of this storm: in the stone-cold center of the airy swirl.

But then Max's coworkers stepped forward and began to speak. The ones at the state housing office. They all admired Max. Perhaps they even loved him. He had helped them when they were in a bind. He did not keep his work to himself but shared. He did not go silent, like too many other colleagues. He spoke up for them and for others. Now they would stand up before this gathering and speak for him.

And soon everything filled the room forming the full outline of Max. He seemed to have been re-created, formed by testimonials and the holy chants of transition so that he was channeled and emerged silently, a silhouette of living light, to keep everyone company. The stories of Max and him together whispered themselves to Finn.

"I remember my first successful act of masturbation."

"What constitutes successful?"

"You know. You finish. And surprising stuff comes out."

"Oh, I thought perhaps you meant getting your actual fantasy girl to materialize in the room. That would be successful masturbation."

"No," Max had said, "that's *Star Trek*."

Summoned by the head nod of a priest who never stopped smiling in a gentle, divine, ace-up-his-sleeve way, Finn now stood mechanically and went to the front of the church. He cleared his throat as if he were in a school play. At least there was no PowerPoint. From the front of the sanctuary he read some psalm or other that sounded like an unconsoling battle cry. Yet just the doing of something, anything, ceremonial in nature mildly soothed him.

Then Finn closed the good book. He spoke of brotherhood, its failings and its tendernesses. He spoke of how Max had been arbitrarily ostracized and taunted and shoved around as a boy, and how Finn, three years younger, had watched it from a distant corner of a hallway or the school yard, in fear and embarrassment, and pretended he didn't even know Max. Finn, a coward, had kept his gaze down, receded, turned his back on Max repeatedly. Perhaps to spare Max the humiliation of knowing his little brother could see all this? But no: it was Finn's own craven vulnerability, shameful shame. He was in countless ways unworthy of Max and his beautiful stoicism. Max's self-designed cool life management system was unpatentable. Max's devotion to the whole enterprise of living even when it didn't meet him halfway. Max's refusal to whine. Max's bursts of compassion for others when he should have, could have, saved all his reserves of compassion for himself. Max suffered terribly but calmly and with complicated knowledge. He was a beautiful brother and although perhaps there were many things the two of them should have said and didn't, should have done but didn't, probably that was the case between all people. He had not been at Max's deathbed. And yet he felt in a way that he had been. He had felt Max depart at his very moment of departure. The mind-meld of brothers had kept them connected. Sometimes when people died it was the vanishing that was so hard. But Max had not really vanished. That would be impossible. There was a growing slur in Finn's words as if he were drunk or deaf or having a mild stroke. He looked out at the congregation and saw some worried faces. He knew then that he sounded insane to absolutely everyone.

In the restaurant afterward, at the reception, people picked at shredded chicken and vinaigretted beans and sat in chairs with their plates in their laps, when there was no room at a table and the manager brought out extra chairs. Max's coworkers from the state office came forward and again praised him to Finn. Both William of the dozen m's and Jonathan of the dozen n's came forward and Jonathan said that at the end it seemed Max had been waiting for someone and that it was probably Finn whom he loved so much, Finn his only brother. Jonathan meant these words as sweet consolation but they were like knitting needles plunged into Finn's ears.

Still Finn was polite and expressed gratitude. He would give them more checks to sign with their secret agent signatures. The afternoon seemed to go on forever and outside he was sure the sun was going down. He hugged the widow, Maureen, his own sister-in-law, whom he no longer disliked. "I'm going to buy an excellent Ouija board," she said.

"There you go," said Finn. But he would take his own grief elsewhere and spend it in the world until it was a thin, tinny pang.

He started to leave the restaurant. The priest and the altar boy were still there hanging around, perhaps waiting to be paid. He had left that to Maureen. He stepped outside, if not completely to leave then at least for air.

He knew philosophers liked to ask why is there something rather than nothing? But death caused one to ask the other question: Why is there now nothing rather than something?

Max's stepson, Dee, came dashing out. "Uncle Finn, come back! Max is here!"

"He's here?"

"Sort of here! You'll be able to feel it," Dee said. "You'll be able to tell."

Sure enough, just as he had felt momentarily during the service, the negative space drawing that had been created through affectionate utterances and stories and feelings and thoughts and surprisingly fond people showing up, all the praise and anecdotes that had formed Max in the church had wandered over to the reception as well. Inside the restaurant, honoring memories had once again conjured his brother as a strong hovering blank watching from above, near the outré chandelier. People had pushed the tables and chairs aside and had begun to dance, pointing at the ceiling as both a dance move and a holy indication. An impromptu deejay was playing what Max had requested: the songs for Max's funeral would be the same songs that he'd chosen for his wedding. "Don't Make Me Over," "Give My Regards to Broadway," "Never Can Say Goodbye," "Monster Mash." Max liked a little range, at the chapel, on the dance floor, in the urn. There should be No Unwanted Symbolism, a dying wish he once had printed on a T-shirt. He also liked wise coffee mugs, his favorite being one that said, EVERYTHING'S SORT OF BULLSHIT. Maureen had had a lot of those made as reception favors.

The music was loud and precluded conversation about the election. All around on the walls the restaurant had removed its usual landscapes of Sicily and Trinidad and allowed for a million photos of Max. Finn walked around with his three-year-old niece saying, "Look at Daddy!" until one of Maureen's sisters came and took the child away. Finn sat back down and absurdly chair-danced a little bit, seated at the perimeter. Then he fell still. No one pulled him up and out to the cleared space for dancing, for which he was grateful. Along with others he swayed in his chair to "They Can't Take That Away from Me," every different version, because there were a lot of versions. *You hold your knife . . . You changed my life.*

"Have you ever noticed how many different covers there are of this song?" said the woman next to him.

"I have," said Finn.

He got up on his own and went over to Maureen, who was looking stranded. He did not even ask her to dance. He just took her hand and she followed. He attempted to move in the celebratory way that others were doing, a dance floor vibe that was supposed to mock death and celebrate life, stepping in a skate fashion, then punching the air and popping out the shoulders with the rest of the crowd. The million photos of Max stared out at him in mild disbelief. Finn grasped Maureen's hand and pulled it to his shoulder then threw his arm around her waist and brought her entire body toward him. All the people who had ever loved him were gone. And in feeling their absence he felt his own self pitted, burnished, caressed, then given a shove off a cliff. He was dancing but clutching, trying hard neither to step on Maureen's toes nor to bury his face in her tawny, odorless hair.

Having returned to the hotel in NoMad, Finn stood alone in the waiting area between the two elevator banks, marking time until a lift came to take him to his room. He supposed he could go into the cocktail lounge for a whiskey but decided instead on the upstairs minibar. He was carrying within himself a huge accumulation of fatigue, and knew that when he got upstairs and placed himself on his bed, he would fall asleep quickly. A minute passed and the light above one elevator lit up green and made its single ding. He stepped into it in the purgatorial way of passengers: his mind bereft, his gaze checked-out; his hands shoved into his trouser pockets. He turned and faced outward in the still-open car, pressed his floor number, then positioned his stare out across the hallway waiting for his elevator to close and move. From here on in perhaps love would seem distant and absurd, like a play he'd gone to as a child. He would move through life and try to think of people gently but without any off-putting specificity. He would seek a consoling patience in the stillness and shiny warping brass of this very elevator, the buttons for its twelve stops each encircled in a moony light with a zodiac of braille beneath the number. He should have had just such a translation for all his clueless gazing at the stars.

He took some tired breaths. Across the corridor, in the opposite bank, a woman got on the elevator directly across from him. She then turned waiting, also facing outward. The two of them looked frozenly at each other.

It was Lily—also in purgatorial, elevator-waiting fashion. She saw him and brightened. Her mouth opened into a flashing, tremulous bite of air, which surely was a smile. All her stabbing familiarity reassembled itself—a crippling thrill in his head. But his door started to close. His hands flew out of his pockets. His fingers fumbled for the hold button on the elevator panel and jabbed at it frantically.

It was too late. Their doors closed, swiping right and left simultaneously, and the floor beneath him began its ascent, pushing against his shoes.

Throughout the fall, winter, and spring there were many such last-minute reversals. First there had been the World Series, when a rain delay halted the momentum for Cleveland and gave the title to Chicago. Then the presidential election, when the candidate with the most votes lost, a somehow perfectly legal botch that even staying up all night—midnight, one a.m., two a.m.—could not repair. Then the Super Bowl, when Atlanta, with the biggest halftime lead of any loser, went on to lose. Later, the Academy Award for Best Picture was given accidentally to the wrong film.

For Thanksgiving Finn had bought a big-bosomed turkey with its entrails jammed down its throat like a mafia kill, then left it in the freezer until Easter, when he caramelized it until the skin turned a butterscotch hue and could be ripped off and eaten like taffy.

The school asked him back for the following year, and Finn said OK but took nothing for granted.

Persistent actuality was often a dulling habit and had to be fought off.

He seemed to be listening too much and too long to Lily's voice on his voicemail. *Is the weather balmy where you are? I'm wondering if the leaves are still on the trees.*

At night sometimes in his dreams, she appeared in her shape-shifting, fata morgana way; they would talk and go places, walking and singing. He was always happy then because it was always good to see her. There was no derangement in her face. Joy— which was now simply an opinion, and one was allowed to have opinions—came to him in this manner with its imperfect aim and odd timing, under- and overshooting, falling short or wide of the mark, too soon, too late, too much. When he looked back at his younger self, he really didn't see in it anyone he knew or anyone who was an actual full being—possibly because he hadn't been studying himself at the time. Of course there were photographs of him and Max and their parents, all of which were lying things.

Sometimes in his dreams they were out to dinner and she would pick at her food. "Why did you order that?" he would ask.

"I forgot what tortellini was," she might say.

He no longer felt the daily need to listen to Lily's voice on his voicemail (*Is the weather balmy where you are? I'm wondering if the leaves are still on the trees.*) and after thirty days had gone by without his playing it the phone company snatched it away forever. "Oh, my god," he said, upon discovering this. He shook the phone as if it were a small box drained of candy. Then he put it back in his jacket pocket, on the inside near his heart. In the air he could feel the radio waves of her voice: Was mankind so stupid as to fail to imagine that the spirit world would naturally learn to take over our antennae, our satellite disks, our cellphone towers?

You were born, he felt, with all emotions already inside. Eventually you would experience each of them. They would pivot one by one and switch on for the first time or the hundredth, and then shut off again and spin, waiting to be called upon for some other event or occasion.

Did we ask too much of life or too little? The dead would have the answer.

"Dunno," she said to him in his dreams, on train tracks or in undulating meadows. Most of his dreams had fields of milkweed or bundle flower. Except the ones that had corridors or train tracks—resituated to give full rein to questions that had hovered then retreated during daylight. "Could be both."

He cleaned out his car, and when he went for drives the smell of spring manure on the farm fields came wafting warmly

at him. Farther out, when he drove between the miles of rape-
seed with its bright, endless yellow, he felt not that he was
encased in acres of agribiz but as if he were in a shockingly new
and golden land.

He saw a songbird winging away in the sky and somehow
knew that it was Lily and understood that his seeing her in the
old way had come at last to an end. All her ingredients and their
assemblage and ligature had detached, fallen back, disappeared.

Still he sometimes felt he and Lily had been organically
reincarnated together all along the great line of time. When she
departed before he did, the problem was simply that he had
to wait too long to join her in the next life, and for him this
resulted in inner tempests and worries about room for potential
error. Perhaps they both had lived in spaces that were halfway
points between childish hope and tired sentimentality, amoral
static and bitter apathy. Periodically he could feel himself plum-
met. His old life seemed a swirl of smoke in a jar. He saw that
no longer caring about a thing was key to both living and dying.
So was caring about a thing.

He knew from the Book of Job that bleakly cursing God
meant you still believed and thus resulted in a gloating God.
So he did not bother. He also knew from the jealousy expressed
in the very first commandment that there were apparently
other gods to investigate, so perhaps he would get around to
doing that. He knew that if you were too critical of religion,
perhaps you were in one. For now he had no good pharmaceu-
ticals nor working philosophy: silence, withdrawal, keeping his
head down, keeping his head up. The drives along bright fields.
The walks around ponds. The sweet uriney smell of the linden
trees. He would become happy to die. He would also become

happy to live. In this way he would never be unhappy again. He was sometimes waiting to say to someone, "You Smug Fuck!" because it would give him a nice jolt to say that to someone, anyone, but the opportunity never arose. He read with stolid wonder the leather-bound cache of letters he had taken from the Tyler inn. He bought a padded envelope to return it all to the innkeeper but then kept forgetting.

He put himself to small tests and tried to love other women but failed. He would sit across from them at restaurants and nod and smile. Paprika might be strewn mesmerizingly like pollen on the cod or the potato salad. Soup steam might moisten his face like dew. Be lighthearted, he would advise himself. Light from the heart reveals the fine print. But nothing kept his mind from wandering. He was like a wren on a roof who, believing the entire house was his, takes off for a moment never to find his way back. The legs and hypotenuses of all the roofs looked the same at most distances.

He was also like a beaver killed by his own gnawed tree.

All yearning and crying out in the dark he had now swept away in order to continue through each day as a stone.

When he looked at other couples, he did not know how they tolerated each other. They had just grown accustomed, he guessed. They had cooked each other. Each was the frog and each was the heated water. Still, he envied them a tiny bit. Their love in pots.

All the best people, it seemed, were on the other side. Perhaps he should hurry there soon himself—before Lily's book group got there. Once that group of bitchcrackers arrived, the afterlife was screwed.

He had once venerated the lives of the saints: pure, in motion.

They would suffer as others were suffering. They would seek the suffering of others. No one would suffer alone. But now it all seemed to him parodic—laced with the satire of a mime. When the March of Dimes sent their postal plea, he tore off the fund-raising dime glued to their literature and put it in his pocket, throwing the paper in the trash. Still, he volunteered at a local hospice to hold the hands of the dying. Day after day, he laid one of his hands on one of theirs. He encircled their wrists with a soft squeeze and sought their pulse. He stroked their arms. He hummed whatever songs popped like minty weeds into his head.

At home at his desk he surfed the web with a dusty board whose circuits often stalled. He refused all cookies. He deleted Melvin H from Ohio. Continually he had to verify online that he was not a robot. He was required to identify traffic lights, taxis, storefronts, crosswalks. Confirm your humanity, was the request. Demonstrate your discernment, your disenchantment, the differential equations of your personhood, the mysterious coordinates of your agitated soul. Why does the hard drive in your chest pound so wonkily? Why are you still here staring? Hashtag: Fixitjesus. Hashtag: Takethewheel. Give us your key and we will let you in. He changed all his passwords to Lily1 with a dozen y's—strong with a long bar of green. Memory. Passage. Nothing in the world was ever truly over.

Acknowledgments

I wish to thank Vanderbilt University, the Cullman Center at the New York Public Library, and the Danish Writers Association for their support. My gratitude as ever goes also to Melanie Jackson and Victoria Wilson.